Praise For Lia Matera
And Laura Di Palma

"The nerves of everyone involved are strung so tight that you wait tensely for the breaking twang."

Chicago Tribune

"Matera's clipped, spare prose thinly disguises the emotional tensions building among her characters."

San Francisco Chronicle

"One of the more interesting new voices in detective fiction . . . a welcome respite from the mystery-by-formula crowd."

The Kirkus Reviews

"Matera skillfully weaves Laura's dissatisfaction with her own circumstances into the investigation of Karen's death, taking a thought-provoking look at the dangers in relationships that grow too close."

Publishers Weekly

Also by Lia Matera
Published by Ballantine Books:

WHERE LAWYERS FEAR TO TREAD
A RADICAL DEPARTURE
THE SMART MONEY
HIDDEN AGENDA
THE GOOD FIGHT
PRIOR CONVICTIONS

A HARD
BARGAIN

Lia Matera

BALLANTINE BOOKS • NEW YORK

Copyright © 1992 by Lia Matera

This book is a work of fiction. Names, characters, places and incidents are either products of the author's imagination or are used fictitiously. Any resemblance to actual events or locales or persons, living or dead, is entirely coincidental.

ISBN 0-345-38059-2

This edition published by arrangement with Simon & Schuster Inc.

Manufactured in the United States of America

First Ballantine Books Edition: April 1993

To BRENDAN REHON
*scientist, naturalist, artist,
riddle-teller, and mess-maker,
with love.*

1

THE CREEK WAS a maze of shallow waterfalls and sudden deep spots, in places unfordable. We dug our toes between wet roots and let the water rush over our rubber boots. We picked our way over horsetailed banks and stream rocks and fallen logs slick with lichen. We sank knee-deep into ooze several shades grayer than the sky. Our conversation shrank to, "This log's rotten, try the rocks," or, "Grab that branch and get back on the bank."

To my cousin it was ordinary, like the rugged homelessness following his release from the veterans' hospital in 1973. It was like the last nineteen years, minus three in the posh apartment we'd given up six months ago.

I glanced at Hal. He was muddy and water-flecked in layers of old sweaters. His salt-and-pepper hair looked windblown and hacked. On one side of him rose a cliff of tangled vines and underbrush, on the other a concave of dripping ferns and rootbound mud. He straddled two submerged rocks, water rushing around his booted ankles. The Colossus of Hicksville. I struggled onto the bank, clutching stalks of broad-leafed cow parsnip.

He watched me with surface disregard. Which irritated

me. I considered trying to force my way under that cuticle. But mornings made Hal feel vulnerable, made him insist on rough hikes in wild terrain to prove he wasn't (still) a handicapped veteran. Later he could pretend his aches and problems were caused by the exertion, he could accept them as part of relaxing by a fire. He could accept needing my company.

My foot slid, and I clung to the bank like a graceless lizard, waiting for Hal's snide remark. No peace-love simplifying for us. This was a hermitage, not a commune.

At times, it was an Outward Bound program: Hal insisting that we tramp and scramble, build bonfires in the rain, as if survival of the clan might someday depend on it.

Whereas we both knew the real basis of our survival. I'd been a high-paid, even famous litigator for most of my adult life. Six months' severance pay and a healthy savings account were our real survival tools—not the ability to ford fast creeks in the rain.

Survival of the clan. A funny concept, in our case. We were second cousins as well as lovers. Grown up far too much in each other's faces, fleeing from one another when we fled our families, reconnecting with a passion when we met again in our early thirties. A cranky damn couple now, almost four years later, living miles from nowhere in a cabin too rustic for me and too fancy for Hal. Trying to avoid Hal's parents as they writhed through their divorce.

I still wasn't sure what had brought us here. Fired from my job, panicked over a recurrence of Hal's war injury, I guess I'd equated reclusion with revival.

"Laura, look up." Hal interrupted my musing.

Just as well. A bad teenage marriage had cured me of constant bone-gnawing reassessment of relationships—until recently. I hadn't put that burden on any of my other postdivorce romances. But I'd had motions to file then, court dates to keep, papers to serve, superiors to appease, clients to protect. And the harrying details of day-to-day life, things I didn't bother with anymore: keeping my wardrobe elegant, my hair tamed, my technology current.

"Laura." Hal's tone was sharper now. "Up there."

I followed his glance to the redwood-shagged crest of the

gorge, a spot not far from where we planned to pull and pant ourselves back to even ground. A spot not far (by country standards) from our cabin.

A person stood there, shirt light against the dark woods. Four hundred miles south, in what most people called "Northern" California, a stranger's silhouette wouldn't cause remark. But Hal and I had hiked this gorge at least once a week, rain or shine, and we'd never encountered another soul. We'd tramped the meadows, squelched through brush, picnicked in thickets of redwood, spruce, and fir—and encountered no one. In six months.

I put a drawl into my voice. "Town folk."

"It's Sandy."

"No way."

"You're not expecting him?"

Like I wouldn't mention it. Such a close friend, someone I'd worked with almost six years. We'd even been lovers for a while.

The figure on the crest waved long arms like semaphores. Because Hal had suggested it, and because I wanted to believe it, I became certain it was Sander Arkelett waving hello.

The last time I saw him, he said I was a fool to walk away from my life to be with a fucking depressive who treated me like shit. I told him to quit casting it as a cheap romance: I'd been fired from my job, damn it. I was burnt out. Sick of the work, sick of the lifestyle. And Hal was not the seething man he became around Sandy; with me he was merely armored.

Through the gorge a call echoed. "Laura!"

I cupped a hand to my mouth and called, "Sandy?" The sound got pulled away by rushing water.

"Fuck that. Let's go up."

I could hear the irritation in Hal's voice. Partly because he still limped on even ground? He seemed especially conscious of it in front of Sandy. He didn't give himself credit: Eight months ago exacerbation of his war injury screwed up movement on his right side. Six months ago, moving here because no plan seemed better, I wouldn't have believed he'd be hiking wild land on his good days, meadows on his bad. Or that I'd be hiking with him, for that matter.

2

By noon, we were showered and warm in flannel permeated with the smell of wood fire. A trayful of bagels and cream cheese hardened on the coffee table.

Sandy nursed a cup of coffee laced with Southern Comfort. He sat forward, legs apart, elbows on his knees, like some elongated Fred Astaire. Sand-colored hair spilled over his narrow, deeply dimpled face. His blue eyes watched the fire at times, me at times. A handsome cowboy. Gary Cooper in city drag.

City clothes—I missed them. Or what I associated with them: being too busy for reflection, demonstrably competent, always accomplishing.

I recalled a news photo of myself in a severely straight-lined Armani, black hair sheared tamely away from my face, features composed to dampen their Italian drama. In flannel and denim, hair a mess of unconditioned curl, I knew I must look different to Sandy— knowing his taste, maybe better. But he knew me too well to think of me as a wild wench, however I might appear today.

We talked a bit, pouring coffee and stoking the fire. Sandy

4

still did investigation for my old law firm. I caught up on the gossip.

But nothing real. So when Sandy got down to it, it seemed without preamble.

"I'm up here on a case. Find out about a lady who killed herself. With a little help."

He fumbled in the pocket of a shirt so baggy I'd never have guessed it contained a cassette. He held the tape aloft, glancing at me inquiringly.

I rose reluctantly from my cushion, tired in the posthike way with which I'd become familiar. I took the tape from Sandy's hand and crossed to the stereo. I could feel Sandy's eyes on me, maybe on the expensive furniture, somewhat incongruous here in the middle of nowhere. (But it was my stuff, no reason to leave it with the dross of my career. And I'd never appreciated it so much—never had the time, never had so little else to do.)

A log cracked into coals, the only sound in the big A-framed room. I snapped the tape into place, hit the play button.

"It's her telephone message tape," Sandy told us. My speakers broadcast a woman self-consciously clearing her throat. "Her outgoing message to whoever called."

"I'm sorry." The voice was tentative, soft. "I've tried to talk myself through this, find a way to stand being in the middle of it. But I see people look at me and I remember when they looked at me because my clothes were nice or my hair just got styled, and I realize that didn't please me either, even though it's what I thought I wanted. In some ways it felt worse, having people look at me because I was primped up. Or sometimes at a party I'd catch a glimpse of myself and think, Wow, I look great, when I'm happy I look beautiful. But it would vanish just like that—my face would change in the split second I stood there looking at it. Because I knew being happy was just a rush, something that would be gone in a minute or an hour. And then I'd be myself again, in the ugly bottom of things, slumped over and gross-faced. It almost seemed dishonest later, when I wasn't happy anymore. Dishonest that I tried to pass myself off as this pretty thing I'm not." A small laugh. "Maybe that's why I . . . used the ice pick. I was sick of hiding the ugliness, I wanted to open myself up and let people see it and hate me for it. Like I do, like I deserve.'' The voice abated for a moment. We listened to the whir of blank tape. ''Ted drives a hard bargain. He puts this gun in front of me every day when he goes to work. It sits here on the kitchen table and I stare at it like I'd stare at a mirror, like it's going to show me something new. I stare at it and all I can think is how naive to believe in choices. Maybe some people have choices; I've got this *thing* inside that snatches me up like a hawk snatching a mouse.'' Another pause. ''I'm going to use the gun. I know what I'm doing and I know it's the best thing.'' A bit defiantly: ''The best thing. So I'm sorry, Ted. I'm sorry, whoever's calling. There's no point leaving me a message.''

A high beep signaled the caller to leave that pointless message.

I glanced at Sandy, wondering why he'd wanted us to hear the tape. Presumably he'd heard it several times already. ''What's the firm's interest?''

For a moment Sandy didn't answer. He was staring at Hal, his head tilted back, his brows lowered consideringly.

Hal was ashen, lips parted, totally still.

Sandy said, ''That's the client's daughter talking. Name of Karen McGuin, age thirty-six. Maiden name Clausen. She was local, went away for a few years, came back. Met this fellow, Ted McGuin, lived together awhile, got married two years ago. Younger guy, thirty. Lives outside Dungeness.'' A small community north of my hometown. ''Then thirteen months ago she tried to kill herself. Slashed both arms and legs with a razor, hacked her face with an ice pick, hacked off part of her nose, screwed up one eye.''

To let people see the ugliness inside, she'd said.

''A razor's bad enough. But an ice pick?'' Imagining it made the tape feel repulsive in my hand. ''Why so ferocious?''

Sandy raised his blond brows. ''Any theories, Hal?''

''Self-hatred,'' he said, his voice as low as it gets.

''Well.'' Sandy made a show of stretching his lean frame. ''Yuh. I'd say that would have to be an element.''

"She recovered?" I was trying to find a tactful way of asking why he'd brought the tape here now.

A wrinkling of the nose. "Looked pretty awful, apparently. But yeah, recovered."

"And then decided to finish what she'd started."

"Since she's been home from the clinics—physical, then mental, then physical—her husband pretty much guaranteed it. That's how it sounds to me."

I handed back the tape. Wanted to press my face to Hal's chest. "He really handed her a gun every morning?"

"Her last words. Sounds like he wanted her to hurry up and finish the job."

Because he knew she was unhappy? Because she looked hideous across the breakfast table? "How exactly—"

Hal interrupted. "The family sent you up here to talk to McGuin?"

"Yuh." A laser glance at Hal. "To him and about him. Thought I could get some background from you."

I don't know which surprised me more, Sandy's statement or Hal's matter-of-fact nod.

3

AN HOUR LATER, the three of us stood at Karen McGuin's grave site. Hal's stubbled cheeks were unusually hollow, his dark brows were pressed into a wince. He looked almost as bad as he had six months ago, before putting aside his cane. I watched his face, not quite admitting tears would make me jealous of the dead woman.

Jealous. A long time since I'd been stupid enough to measure myself by how much other people loved me. It wasn't practical, not in my line of work. And it certainly wasn't consoling. Not with a taciturn lover like Hal.

Maybe it was a function of being back in my hometown: verging on emotions I thought I'd burned to cinders as a teenage wife with no reason to think well of myself and too much invested in what other people—my then husband—thought of me. Here, in a town I'd superstitiously avoided for most of my adult life.

I'd been back only twice. Once four years ago. Hal had been here then too, his first visit in thirteen years. He'd booked himself into an abandoned housing project—more than arm's length from his father, the mayor. I'd been too full of myself and my own schemes to wonder what brought

Hal back. Turned out it was the woman upon whose grave he now squatted.

It was a multiple grave site, slabs of cement showing placement of caskets in a concrete bed designed to keep mourners out of Pacific Northcoast mud. In two buckling rows were the woman's great-grandparents, grandparents, and an uncle killed in World War II. A tiny, sodden Memorial Day flag was wedged into a crack beside his grave. There was room for three more graves in that concrete parcel, not enough for the woman's survivors. But her husband would probably be buried elsewhere—a husband who'd conspicuously placed a loaded gun on the kitchen table every morning when he left for work. Every morning since her return from the last hospital, still and permanently disfigured.

The cemetery was atop a hill in Dungeness, a small dairy town five miles inland from the dead woman's home. From where we stood, I could see spruced Victorians and a downtown of false-front former feed stores, now retouched and stocked with antiques and starving galleries. Around it, dairy country, sodden and green, spread toward Highway 101. My hometown, ten miles south, was the nearest "city," its population having dwindled from thirty to twenty-five thousand after lumber mill closures and a decade of bad fishing; not enough cash in those lean pockets to support a neighbor's redwood sculptures and Art Nouveau fribbles.

Sandy turned away from the grave, shading his eyes from the bright white sky as he scanned the town. "What the fuck are you doing *here*?"

I shifted closer to him. "Why not here?"

"Damn it, Laura." His tone was kinder than his words. "Steve Sayres would rehire you. All you have to do is ask. They brought in two associates don't get half your work done."

"Sayres would never give me the latitude Doron did. And he's pissed at me. He'd punish me with a bunch of routine debt collection."

Three times I'd insisted on taking high-impact, pro bono criminal cases. Twice Doron White, senior partner of the elegantly corporate White, Sayres & Speck, had gotten swept into my adrenaline rush, shielding me from his partners' fiscal outrage. The third time, Doron sided with them and I got fired. But Sandy was right. With Doron dead of a heart attack, the firm needed rainmakers. It would take me back if I promised to be a good girl and stick to civil practice.

"Plenty of other firms in the city would hire you. You know that—they'll be talking about the Wallace Bean case for a hundred years."

Wallace Bean, assassin of two United States senators, had been my highest-profile client. Winning his acquittal had made me famous. Unfortunately, Bean ended up dead in an alley, shot by an indignant vigilante.

Sandy plucked my sleeve. "And here you are playing Walden Pond."

"This isn't forever."

"It's been half a goddamn year already." He inclined his chin toward the row of former feed stores at the foot of the hill. "This is what you're settling for? What you went to law school for?"

"I didn't go to law school to get fired right before I made partner." It still rankled. I changed the subject. "So why are you involved in this case?"

Sandy tucked his hands into his anorak pockets, squinting down at me. "D.A. won't bring criminal charges. There's not enough motive evidence, apparently. Not even for manslaughter."

"What about accessory? Suicide's a crime; the husband abetted a felony. Or how about conspiracy to commit a felony?"

"Problem's proving what he had in mind. Or that putting the gun on the table's what made her kill herself. I assume that's the D.A.'s hang-up."

"Bullshit. Isn't there a more aggressive D.A. in that office?"

He grinned. An old inside joke: when it came to my cases, no one seemed aggressive enough to me.

"They may have Attila the Hun in there, but the lady working on this case says no go. And that sticks in the family's craw. They want me to talk to people who know the husband, try to nail down proof of motive to give the D.A."

I felt Hal's hands on my shoulders as he spoke. "He put

a loaded gun in front of someone who was just getting over a suicide attempt. Why isn't that proof enough?''

"If it were aggressively investigated and argued—''

"In and of itself, why isn't it proof?'' His tone was clipped, almost hostile.

Sandy and I exchanged glances. We were longtime coworkers. He knew how weary it made me, explaining the difference between what's fair and what's legal. It usually made people angry, made them beat me up with how things *should* be. What difference did it make how things should be?

"The elements required to prove criminal conduct are necessarily stringent. Since the sanctions are—''

Hal's grip on my shoulders tightened. "Why are you patronizing me?''

"I'm not.''

His hands slid off me. I shivered, missing their warmth.

Below us, wet dairyland presented a more pleasing reality. Cows gave milk or they didn't, without moral ambiguity.

Sandy said, "Laura, a favor? Come talk to the husband with me?''

"Why?''

"Make sure I don't miss some legal nuance.''

Old times. "I'm out of lawyer mode, Sandy.''

"We're talking about an hour of your time, Laura.'' He didn't look at me, continued squinting at the farms. "Unless you've got some pressing engagement.''

"You don't need me. Look at me.'' Toe to toe. "Look at me, Sandy. What's this about? Really.''

I prepared anger, expecting a call to take up legal cudgels again. To my annoyance, Sandy grinned. "I miss you like hell, you know that?''

I heard Hal, still behind me, turn and walk away.

Sandy spared him a glance before continuing. "If the D.A. won't prosecute, the family might sue—civil case, wrongful death or something. So two things I'd like to get out of the husband today. What was his wife depressed about last year, and was she depressed about the same thing this year? Independent of husband putting the gun out there.''

"You don't need me.''

"We're a good team—I'd like your input. I'd like to know what you think of the husband. If you think he's being honest."

"Want me to introduce you to him?" Hal had rematerialized behind me.

Sandy's head jerked back. "Didn't know you knew him. What I heard was you knew her."

"Him too."

I turned, expecting Hal to say more. He looked down at me. That's all. Trust Hal to leave it at that.

4

T ED McGUIN'S LOOKS were almost shocking in our lily-white backwoods. His broad face was paper bag brown, his eyes were almond-shaped and moss green, his hair was dark chocolate, cut close, very curly. He had a trimmed mustache sprinkled with blond and red hairs that further testified to a mixed heritage. His expression was intense and inward, reminding me of a jazz musician I'd seen on some old album cover. He was powerfully built, might have been intimidating if he hadn't been short, just an inch or two taller than me. But the most striking thing about him was a wide smile that deeply crinkled the skin around his eyes. That trick of facial muscles either reflected or gave the illusion of warmth and genuineness.

I'd tell Sandy to warn his clients. The man had a smile guaranteed to touch cold jurors.

I reminded myself that he'd placed a loaded gun in front of his suicidal wife day after day until she blew away what was left of her face.

He was standing in the yard of a tiny house with a huge view of rocky coast. He was encased in a black wet suit, outer jacket unzipped, about to hoist a scuba tank onto his

13

back. He was smiling at a kitten that batted his hand as he reached for the gear.

"Silly-ass cat." A surprisingly deep voice. "Don't bite anything you can't eat, don't you know that? Hmmm?" The kitten furiously gnawed his finger.

I caught Sandy's eye. Sandy grinned. The man certainly looked like a wife killer.

Hal stepped forward. "Ted."

McGuin took a startled step backward, thigh muscles bunching visibly in their neoprene sheath. "Youch!" he cried, pulling the kitten off his now raised hand.

"You remember me?"

"Hal. Hi." His brows sank. "I guess you heard." He set the kitten down, looking first at me, then at Sandy.

"This is Sandy Arkelett. He's a detective working for Karen's family. He wants to talk to you about what happened."

Ted McGuin sighed, his upper body curling slightly. He peeled off the jacket of his wet suit, hanging it inside out over his scuba tank.

Hal continued. "And this is my . . . this is Laura."

McGuin glanced at me, folding his bare arms over his chest. The remaining neoprene was cut like an overall, skin-tight and glossy over smooth brown skin.

Sandy said, "I'd really appreciate a short chat. The family'd like some details. You know how it is."

"The family," McGuin said carefully, "knows my phone number."

"You know how it is," Sandy repeated.

I felt a surge of affection for Sandy. I'd always liked the way he worked: addressing concerns with empty phrases designed to keep the conversation flowing while revealing nothing. For a minute I missed my work, missed the gamesmanship.

"Right." McGuin's baritone became a shade less friendly. "They don't want to be talking to black people if they can help it. Even relatives by marriage."

"Really?" Sandy appeared surprised, perhaps even genuinely. "I don't get that impression from them."

A glimpse of McGuin's smile. "Why would you?"

Beyond his bit of weedy yard, the terrain dropped, showing a path beaten through lush scrub to a cove flanked by rocks. The morning drizzle had burned off and it was almost warm out. The ocean swells were high and opaque, without whitecaps. The Hillsdale *Union-Messenger* called this a "Mediterranean" July—weather in the midsixties and calm seas.

I wondered what it looked like under the surface, what McGuin envisioned when he looked at the water. My mind's eye saw a swirling broth of sand and plankton, rocks padded with flat purple anemones and streamered with kelp. A scene from some old Cousteau special, surely. I glanced at McGuin and found him watching me; had the disconcerting feeling he'd put that picture in my head, slipped a frame of his consciousness into mine.

"It's amazing under there," he said. Then he blinked, looking a little nonplussed himself. "Well, you guys are welcome to come in. I don't know what the family wants to know, but I'll talk to you."

He led us stiffly across the yard, his neoprene-bootied feet shoulder distance apart, suggesting the king of Siam.

We walked through the open back door and into a tidy old-fashioned kitchen of linoleum squares and flecked Formica. A round wood table, scarred but oiled, dominated the room. He'd placed a loaded gun there every morning.

McGuin stood in the middle of the room, staring at the table, buffing his curls.

I heard a long sigh from Hal.

"So what happened?" Sandy's voice was sympathetic.

"What started out as occasional depression . . . ." He stood frozen, still staring at the table. "It took over. More and more."

"Not related to anything that was happening to your wife at the time?" Sandy managed to sound a little skeptical while maintaining a generally sympathetic tone.

"Have you ever dived?" He looked up at Sandy, his eyes suddenly bright.

"No."

"It's like being in a huge pot of soup. You have to accept that you're going to bob around, get buffeted around." He demonstrated, taking a few quick steps left, a couple right, his arms raised slightly. "You have to compensate for it. If you're going this way and you get swept left a bit, you jag over gradually, compensating, yeah, but also not getting hung up on going to an exact spot on the rock. Once you're there, you can pull yourself to spot X, but in the meantime you have to learn to like the feeling of being part of the soup, you have to like the game of getting around in the soup."

Hal touched the tabletop. I felt a prickle of irritation and knew Sandy shared it. You have to be careful when people are talking not to dam their flow. To bob in the conversational soup.

McGuin was distracted. "You heard what she said about the gun."

Hal said, "Yes."

Sandy tried to recover the thread. "Your wife didn't follow the drift?"

"I tried to teach her to dive, but man . . . She either fought it like hell, or she didn't compensate at all and let it pull her away. She was dangerous to go out with."

Sandy was about to encourage him to elaborate. We'd found, over the years, that metaphors didn't always play out as we expected.

But Hal interjected, "Why did you—?"

"Who are you exactly?" McGuin was scrutinizing Sandy, his wide eyes narrowed. "Are you a friend of the family, or what?"

Damn. Sandy could have deferred this moment. The question was inevitable, but I'd seen Sandy play so skillfully it didn't come up till he was ready to leave. He was far better at initial questioning than I was. I was too blunt. If I wasn't careful, women got competitive, men got threatened. Sandy had a lighter touch, an easier manner.

On the other hand, I was the better adversary. With Sandy's finessed secrets, I was hell in depositions.

I felt a sentimental surge—not typical of me until about my fourth vodka. Half a year away from Sandy. From the game.

"You mind if we sit down?" Sandy wanted things relaxed—as relaxed as possible, considering the news he was about to break.

McGuin gestured his assent. Stood for a moment after we sat.

Sandy waited for him to join us. Then he said, "The way her suicide came down . . ." A friendly shrug. "You can understand how it sounds to the family."

"Yeah, well, things aren't always how they sound."

"That's all," Sandy said. "They need to understand."

Here it got tricky. As a lawyer—long time since I'd thought of myself that way—I'd feel obligated to mention that the family might sue. A clean, trick-free record. That's why I'd often let Sandy do the initial questioning for me in situations where I wanted as much information as possible. (With clients, as opposed to witnesses, I did my own questioning; cuing them that some facts should remain unuttered.)

"So you're a friend of the family?" McGuin looked solemn, even in neoprene long johns. A face that could be South American, Sicilian, South African "colored." A unique ethnicity his in-laws apparently did not value.

Sandy glanced at me. I wondered if he'd lie to McGuin if I weren't present. I'd seen him cross that boundary of professionalism; I'd seen him commit assault to get what he wanted, in fact. The legacy of a six-year stint with the Los Angeles police.

"I work for a fellow named Sayres," Sandy admitted. "Your wife's family asked him to get this information for them." Sandy's quiet concern was undercut by an annoyed glance at Hal.

He obviously hadn't wanted to bring Sayres into it—hadn't wanted McGuin to get the right impression. "A fellow named Sayres"—made Steve sound like a country boy, a sole practitioner. Not the senior partner in a big San Francisco firm. Not the shark in fine worsted that he was.

But Sayres was a cautious, by-the-book lawyer. I should know; I'd worked for him almost seven years. He'd want this interview as aboveboard as possible; wouldn't want it coming out in deposition that Sandy had outright lied.

"We'd like to put the family's minds at rest," Sandy concluded. "That's all."

McGuin frowned, polishing the tabletop with his knuckles. "No way you're going to do that—I know them. As well as they let me. And from what Karen told me. From how they treated her.''

"How did they treat her?'' There was an urgency I didn't understand in Hal's question.

"They just want to know.'' Sandy tried to steer the conversation back. I could feel his desire to muzzle Hal.

"No, they don't.'' McGuin's lips pinched. "They're trying to get me arrested, aren't they?''

"No, no.'' Sandy held up a reassuring hand. "Steve Sayres isn't a criminal lawyer.''

"Then what? They're suing me? Trying to get the house away? What?''

"At this stage, they're looking for information. Hell, their daughter died. And you've got to admit, it looks damn cold, what she says you did. They want to know why.''

"Bullshit. They want to sue my ass.'' He stood, leaning forward so that his fingertips touched the table. "Tell them they can sue me and they can think whatever narrow—'' He leaned heavily on the fingertips, his breathing ragged and audible. "I don't give a flying fuck if it looks cold.''

"I do.'' Hal's voice was steely.

The corners of McGuin's mouth tightened. He kept his eyes fixed as they filled with tears.

"Let's just mellow out.'' Sandy's voice was soothing. "Di Palma, why don't you step outside for a few?''

Hal sat immobile.

I reached across the table, sliding my hand over his forearm. "Five minutes, Hal.''

He jerked his arm away. Stood angrily. Looked at me for a stony second before leaving.

I'd done it again.

"If you need a while—want to get a robe or whatever?'' Sandy's tone was gentle, not at all patronizing. I envied that skill. "Glad to make you some coffee or tea, if you don't mind offering us some.''

We sat there maybe two minutes. McGuin stared at the tabletop, his torso curling as he hugged himself. Tensed, his arms were huge, knotted with muscle that lacked definition; genetic not gymnastic.

He finally said, "It's too complicated. Just go away.''

"Give us a chance." I'd retained the habit of insistence. "We haven't got an agenda, we just want to hear your side."

Instant regret: of course "we" had an agenda. And what side could he present? That it was hard being tethered to a maimed woman's mental illness?

"I don't need to give 'my side,' okay? I don't need to do that." He stepped back abruptly. "And I don't know anyone I think deserves that from me. Especially not Karen's family."

He stalked out of the kitchen, elbows out and head bowed, as if picking his way over rough coral.

5

CONSIDERING I'D MADE my living as a litigator, I found it surprisingly exhausting to spar with Hal. He seemed determined not to hear what I was saying. I repeated myself.

"It's a matter of the facts—those available to the D.A. at this point—not fitting the legal definition of murder. I'm not saying that's good or fair or whatever. I'm saying the legal definition can't cover every situation. If it was broad enough to cover just putting a weapon at someone else's disposal, you'd have parents pulled in for their kids' vehicular homicides."

"No." Hal's voice was cold. Probably his expression was colder, but he bent over the hearth, building a fire we needed in this sunless redwood thicket. "Putting a gun in front of someone who's suicidal is like lending your car to a drunk."

"Calm down, Di Palma. She's just giving the D.A.'s position." Sandy knew how to light Hal's tinder.

"What McGuin did—how's it different from pulling the trigger himself?"

I restated the obvious: "Because he didn't pull the trigger."

"The state of mind she was in, the hell he didn't." Hal

struck a match, dropping it onto the bed of paper. "He basically said, 'You're deformed now: Die.' "

Sandy's drawl cut in. "We don't know that yet. We don't know what was on his mind."

One of the things that made Sandy a good detective was his willingness to reserve judgment. Refusing to embrace a pet theory, he explored more options.

Hal saw it differently. "Get so hung up on legalistic definitions you can't see the obvious reality."

"It's not a matter of reality." My voice climbed in pitch. "There's moral reality, psychological reality. We're talking legal. Legal definitions create the legal reality. Obviously. Why is that concept so amazing?"

"What's amazing"—an over-the-shoulder glance—"is that you're still so invested in it."

"The D.A.'s invested in it. And I recognize it—like I'd recognize a weather pattern. I'm not saying it's how I'd order my utopia. I'm telling you how it is, and you're mad because it's not how you think it should be."

"Yeah, well maybe you wouldn't be so entrenched in the immutable correctness of the law if you'd known Karen."

"Fuck." After my legal contortions on Wallace Bean's behalf, the public excoriations of my groundbreaking defense, the subsequent Senate bill outlawing it.

"Immutable correctness, my behind." Sandy's tone was flat, almost bored. "She's just saying we've got the law on one side, a few facts on the other. We get enough facts, maybe they'll fit the formula. Maybe they won't."

Hal poked the fire a few times. "And Karen falls between the cracks."

"Maybe, maybe not."

"Whatever happened to 'aggressive' litigation?" He didn't need to look at me to needle me with my hubris.

"It's not my case." Facile—and therefore common—to tar all lawyers with the same brush.

"So who was Karen?" Sandy's tone had an undercurrent of, What makes her so damn important?

"You asking? Or is that a rhetorical put-down?"

Hal and Sandy didn't like each other, never had. But communication between them had never been so unvarnished by amenities.

"I'm asking. What was she like?"

"Teasing. Laughed a lot."

I felt my shoulder muscles knot. Men didn't get into teasing relationships with women they weren't bedding. I had a mental glimpse of Hal laughing a lot.

He didn't laugh a lot with me.

"What was she depressed about, do you know?" Sandy's tone was mollifying; he wanted information now, not reaction.

Hal turned away from the fire, finally facing us. "Last time we were up here, what, three and a half years ago?"

Four years ago. At that time I hadn't been back to my hometown in fourteen years, Hal hadn't been back in almost that long. We hadn't seen each other in eight. I'd returned to settle some matters with my ex-husband. Sandy had come along to keep me company. I couldn't remember wondering why Hal had returned.

"I was living up in Vancouver," Hal continued. "I heard from someone that Karen was flipping out. That she was with this younger guy, and it wasn't working."

Sandy sat up straight. "You came down here to see Karen? Back when I first met you? That's why you were here? To see Karen McGuin?"

"Karen Clausen," Hal corrected.

I felt a sudden consternation. I'd never asked Hal why he came back, and he'd never volunteered the information. Were we really so aloof?

"So yeah? What did you hear exactly?"

Hal looked at Sandy, face cold and remote, apparently deciding whether to answer, whether it was Sandy's business. Or maybe knowing it was Sandy's job and not wanting to help.

"I heard she wasn't answering calls, wasn't going out. This was right after she met McGuin; people cut her some slack for a while—figured she was caught up in the romance. But it got to the point where they were worrying. They'd go by the house and she wouldn't answer the door, she'd peek out the curtain, hide till they left."

"And you came down here because of that?" Sandy sounded skeptical.

"The timing was right." A brief glance at me. "Relationship I was in, it was ending. I needed to go."

The relationship he was in. Yes, he'd been prickly and paranoid, full of transferred hostility and bitter comments about women. Part of me wanted details. Part of me wanted to forget I knew this much.

"So did you see Karen Mc—Clausen when you got down here?"

"I went over there when McGuin was at work. She wouldn't let me in at first. I could hear her in the house, shuffling near a window—almost sounded like a mouse. I went over to where the sound was coming from and I started talking about some times we had." A fleeting smile. "She finally let me in."

After a moment Sandy said, "So? Was she okay?"

"I guess so, I don't know."

"Sounds like you're apologizing. Who to?"

The look Hal shot Sandy was hostile.

Sandy stretched languidly. We might have been discussing the price of turnips.

For a while the three of us watched the fire, a huge pyre in a hearth big enough to roast a boar. Big enough to take the chill off a "Mediterranean" summer.

It hadn't been easy finding a "cabin" remote enough to feed my sudden longing for hermitry, yet luxurious enough not to shock me out of the desire. It hadn't been easy finding a place worthy of my cozy furniture, with plank and brick walls to accent my artwork.

Sandy broke the silence. "Gather you met McGuin?"

"Yeah. I stayed for dinner. McGuin came home, fucking full of himself, talking nonstop about his day at work. Output only. Karen might as well have disappeared." A brutal poke at the fire caused a log to fall, sending smoke and ash into the room.

"He say anything germane?"

"No."

"How'd he act around her?"

Hal shrugged. "Like I said, full of himself."

Sandy remained in languid repose, but I could feel his interest. McGuin's attitude toward his wife would be key to proving later animus.

"How'd he treat her?"

A grudging shrug.

"Mind elaborating?"

The look they exchanged confirmed my suspicion of an animosity beyond obvious explanation. It wasn't just territory or personality, it wasn't just me.

Sandy looked away first. "Laura, feel like talking to some folks at the hospital?"

Trying to pull me back into what he still thought of as "our" job? "About her medical condition?"

"Partly. Partly McGuin—he's an emergency room medical tech; find out what his supervisors think of him. Lady in charge is a friend of yours. You could get me an entrée."

Last time I saw the "lady in charge" at County Hospital, Sandy was being wheeled into an operating room; Wallace Bean's vigilante had shot him, too. "We haven't been friends for twenty years."

"But you were friends in high school. I'm just a nosy outsider."

"Don't sell yourself short," Hal grumbled. "All your folksy charm."

I hastily agreed to accompany Sandy, hoping to avert an escalation of tension. Or maybe I wasn't used to strife anymore.

The possibility chilled me. I need my calluses.

6

MADELEINE ABRUZZI SMILED a trifle coolly and said, "We did have some crazy ideas back then."

To me it seemed crazy that a miniskirted teenager given to eruptions of Francophilia should become a grim-faced administrator in tight polyester. Crazy that a talented pianist should be dissuaded from trying Juilliard and now boasted she'd never set foot outside California. France? And affronted, Oh no, her family came first. And she'd heard they were so unfriendly there.

I looked around an austere office that stank of hospital disinfectant. Surely no environment could be more unfriendly than this.

Sandy, seemingly relaxed and loose-limbed, showed signs of tension: a small crease between his brows, a fixedness of smile. I was supposed to be softening up County Hospital's administrative nurse, not antagonizing her. Discussing high school was not having the desired effect. Maybe because I'd gotten where I wanted to be, confounding smug predictions that a teenage marriage meant mortgaging my dreams to housework and babies. Whereas Madeleine Abruzzi had convinced herself she'd been "crazy" to want more than an eight-by-ten office and the right to boss a few nurses around.

"So tell me about your job. Is it totally administrative, or do you still deal with patients?"

"If we're extremely short-staffed, I make myself available." She sat stiffly, her face white from sucking in a spreading torso. The first thing she'd said when I walked in was that I didn't look much different. She'd spoken in pique, daring me to draw conclusions from her extra pounds. "Primarily I oversee the staff."

"Including Ted McGuin."

"Unfortunately." She scowled. "I don't see why nothing's been done about him."

"Yuh?" Sandy's encouraging syllable may not have been necessary.

"If the rumors are true, anyway."

"What rumors?"

"That he gave his wife a gun and told her to finish killing herself." Sudden spots of color on her cheeks reminded me of the French-spouting, arm-waving girl she'd once been. "I probably shouldn't even say that. It's probably libel."

Slander. "Not if it's true. Do you know if it is?"

"Several people have said so."

"From personal knowledge?"

Sandy shot me a look. I should have let her go with it, not rush in for a lawyer's definition. Damn, I was rusty.

"And also, it's easy to see the sheriff's theory from the kinds of questions he asked." A sly glance. "Jay Bartoli, Laura. Remember him?"

Before I could reply, Sandy jumped in. "We've told you who we work for. So you know we'd like to find out what the sheriff asked." A verbal bow to her intelligence; appealing to the vanity that made her mention deducing the sheriff's theory. "And my job aside, I think it's important this get settled. I think the more people clear the air, the better for everyone."

Madeleine nodded. "If Ted did that to his wife, he deserves trouble. It's nothing short of spousal abuse."

Spousal abuse? That seemed a mild assessment.

"So what's the story on McGuin? You people see him at work; you know him as well as anyone."

"I don't see him as often as the emergency room and floor nurses. But from my experience, he seems enthusiastic and cheerful. We've had a problem with him wanting to do more than his training certificate allows him to do."

"Like what?"

"Inserting catheters, charting. He even asked to do stitching once when we had mass casualties. Not necessarily that he's incompetent to do those things, or that we don't have to look the other way in an extreme emergency—we're grateful sometimes for a little initiative—but in terms of our insurance coverage, he's not supposed to do certain things, and I've had to talk to him about it."

"Is he well liked?"

"He was. A couple of the older nurses have complained that his talk's . . . not scandalous. How did they put it? Peppery? I don't know exactly what they meant. Profanity maybe. Sexual references. You see a lot in this job, and there's a tendency to get a little . . . relaxed."

"Anything else the nurses mention?"

"Not really. We talked about him the two times his wife came in to get stitched."

Sandy sat straighter. "Stitched? Before the suicide attempt?"

"About a year before. Twice, maybe three months apart. I had to work in the E.R. one of the times, we were so short-staffed. I remember that time very well. She had a cut on her abdomen, long but not very deep. She'd apparently fallen holding a knife. I guess she didn't think it was bad. She waited hours to come in and get it taken care of. Ted seemed very upset. He'd gotten off work, gone home, and had to turn back and bring her in. He was asking the docs about possible inner-ear fluid imbalances and the like—loss-of-balance problems. That was the second time. She had another cut, pretty much healed, higher up." Her face protracted with remembered concern, making her look almost amphibious. "I wasn't there the first time, but I heard it was the same. Ted brought her in after he went home."

"Didn't you think it was odd, same thing happening twice?"

"Yes. The doctor was very concerned about Karen's balance. But the tests came out negative."

"Could the cuts have been self-inflicted? Dress rehearsal for her suicide?"

Madeleine seemed to consider my face millimeter by millimeter, as if I were a lizard in a terrarium.

"They could have been." Her tone was crisp. Professional. "I couldn't give you a definitive answer."

Sandy honeyed his voice. "What's the word among the nurses?"

"The nurses felt sorry for them, for both of them. Ted was obviously very upset."

"She did her convalescence here, didn't she, after her suicide attempt?"

"She was here less than a week. Her injuries were terrible in terms of looks, but they weren't life-threatening, not after we stopped the bleeding. It was just a matter of keeping the wounds dressed. As soon as she stabilized, they transferred her to M.H.U.—the mental health unit across the street. The reconstructive work on her face was done here too. But that was just a couple of overnights."

"Did she say anything might interest us? That you know of?"

Madeleine leaned forward in her padded secretary chair, forearms crossed on the desk. "When the call came over the wire and we found out it was Ted's wife, several of us were waiting for the ambulance. Besides the regular E.R. staff. So I was there when the medics brought her in. She talked a little bit then. The doc was asking her some questions to see if she was alert and oriented." Madeleine's brow pinched. She looked me in the eye. "She said she couldn't keep her end of the bargain. Her exact words: her end of the bargain. I have no idea what she meant by that."

7

"So." SANDY GLANCED at me, relaxing into the gray vinyl of his rented Nissan.

It felt funny to be driven. Hal didn't drive anymore—wasn't supposed to anyway—and I liked not having to balance politeness against a stubborn preference to choose my own route, go my own speed.

"So?"

"I'd say Abruzzi gave us mixed signals. Everyone including her used to like McGuin fine—except now they want him hung up by the nuts for killing his wife."

"They definitely think he killed her."

"With animus."

I thought about the man we'd watched play with a kitten. "I don't get the relationship between him and his wife."

"Hoping your cousin could help us with that one." Sandy's tone made it clear the hope had been scotched.

"Hal's not one to analyze relationships." I was startled by the hint of bitterness. I didn't need to get touchy-feely either. I wasn't the type.

"Doesn't like McGuin much."

"No."

"Obviously had some kind of relationship with the wife once." Sandy's tone was carefully neutral.

I let it go. I watched Victorians scroll past the windshield: grand old houses, well maintained but not precious, too common here to be gussied like rarities. "Where are we going?"

Until this year, Hillsdale had seemed a small town to me. Until this year, I'd never lived out in the country. Never wanted to.

"Talk to the family."

"His or hers?"

"His first, then hers."

"Okay."

I didn't belong with him on the interviews, questioned his motives for taking me. But I didn't have anything better to do.

I felt his hand cover mine. I looked at him and found him grinning at me. I grinned back.

We drove through stately old neighborhoods of Victorians flanked by rhododendrons as big as fruit trees. As we approached the bay, lawns became less manicured and driveways more crowded: houses had been carved into small rentals. By the time we reached the marina, the afternoon sky was white and a pillow of fog smothered the bay. On either side of us, former flophouses and rough bars had been chichied with false fronts and stained glass, newly bricked walkways had been cleared of derelicts, small breweries and galleries kept lights burning for the nonexistent foot traffic.

"McGuin's family lives here?"

"Address I have is on Two Street."

"That used to be the worst street in town. Drunk fishermen and old winos."

"How long ago?"

"I'm not sure." I'd stayed gone so long. "Six, seven years?"

Sandy stopped the car in front of a two-story box with a peaked roof and sagging porch. Bare wood showed through the remains of white paint, changing the shade to gray.

"I guess it missed getting yuppified," Sandy said.

We climbed out of the car, inhaling fog tainted with the hint of pulp mill and fishery. Houses up and down the block looked like impressively primped versions of this one. A few sported historic landmark plaques.

Sandy knocked on the door, saying, "Curtains closed—might not be home."

I glanced at the curtains, then stepped closer. Strips of velvet, silk, and brocade in mossy greens and rich purples had been cross-stitched together. The patterns were complementary in unexpected ways.

My reverie was broken by the door opening and a woman lamenting, "Oh! You're not who you're supposed to be!"

She was a tall, fair-skinned redhead, maybe fifty years old, a little heavy in jeans and sweatshirt. When Sandy smiled, she smiled too, eyes squinting and dimples peeping girlishly.

"Well, I don't know who I'm supposed to be, but I can tell you who I am."

The woman laughed for a tinkling second that ended in a smoker's cough. "Well, how many people can say that? Don't even ask me who I'm supposed to be. Georgia O'Keeffe." Suddenly and self-consciously, she stuck out her hand. "I'm Hannah Arthur. Hello, how do you do?"

"I'm Sandy Arkelett and this is Laura Di Palma."

"Are you here to buy clothes?"

"No." Sandy looked amused. "Is what I'm wearing okay?"

The woman shook her head, a Gibson girl chignon threatening to slide out of its pins. "Very boring. My sister and I make clothes—"

"Wearable art," said a voice behind her.

Both women laughed.

"Clothes," the redhead repeated. "As you can see, it's not Wyatt."

Almost in unison they grunted a disappointed "Oh." I heard retreating footsteps.

"Um," Sandy seemed somewhat at a loss. "We represent Karen McGuin's family."

I watched Hannah Arthur's face. She suddenly looked nearer sixty than fifty.

"Family's very troubled," he continued. "As you can imagine. They basically hired me to ask the kind of questions they'd be uncomfortable asking."

"And you are what?" Delicate fingers fluttered to her lips as if expecting to find a cigarette there. "A lawyer?"

"Ms. Di Palma's the lawyer. I'm an investigator."

Hannah Arthur's sister returned to the door, this time where I could see her. Although fairly light-skinned, she was definitely black, with long crimped hair caught in a braid and huge brown eyes. When she stood beside her sister, the family resemblance was evident. But features one assumed were "white" on a pale redhead looked African on a woman with dark skin. She was more dressed up than Hannah, in knit tunic and pants with most of the life washed out of them. And she carried her excess weight in a roundly compact way. Although heavier than her sister, she looked like she'd be firmer to the touch.

"I gather one of you is Ted McGuin's mother?"

The sister answered. "I am." Her voice was soft, a little raspy. The smell of tobacco shrouded her.

"Sandy Arkelett." He stuck out his hand. "I don't know how else to do this. I know it must be hard for you. I hope you'll understand that it's hard for Karen's family, too. And that knowing more about the situation will hopefully make it easier for them."

"Since when does information do that?" McGuin's mother spoke a little haltingly, maybe shyly. "Usually the more you know, the more complicated and impossible it all gets." Her eyes were liquid with some emotion. "I'm Sarah Gowan."

"Could we come in and talk?"

The sisters exchanged glances, parted their lips as if to speak, frowned as if thinking better of it. Not quite in unison, but close.

As Sarah Gowan said, "Okay," and looked away from us, her sister made a sound approaching "ow." Definitely miffed, either at us for intruding or at Sarah for allowing us to enter.

We stepped into a room of shabby furniture and immense frames of fabric art, some propped against walls, some hung on tapestry rods. I heard Sandy murmur something about quilts without stuffing, but he was wrong. Quilts were folk art. These were more: slivers of shine, swatches of color, raised patterns, needlework, batik, shapes that were elusively more than one thing, resonant with West African colors.

"These are wonderful." My blurted remark elicited no reaction. Apparently the women didn't need me to like their work. Either they liked it beyond insecurity, or the opinion of a stranger meant little to them. Good thing; judging from the threadbare old furniture and the faded rug, their art barely supported them. Maybe I knew how they felt: the only real artistry in which I'd engaged had been pro bono.

Both women lit cigarettes. Sarah sat cross-legged on the floor staring at hers; Hannah stood hand on hip, taking quick drags and exhaling noisily. She spoke first.

"No, we can't help you, we really can't. Because we've discussed it, you see. All Karen's pain. Like a mirror. No, no, we really can't face it now."

Sandy looked a little perplexed. "You mean to say it hurts to talk about it?"

"Denial, we're in pure denial. Go ahead and prove it even happened, buster." Another peep of dimple as strands of auburn hair slid free of their pins. Then her face crumpled and her eyes welled with tears.

"We were very close." Sarah Gowan looked up from the burning tip of her cigarette. "She was like . . ." Her wet eyes searched the wall. "Like the velveteen in that wall hanging—so shiny you'd think it's metallic. But softness is what gives it that sheen. And it's very hard to work with velveteen— it crushes so easily."

Hannah blinked her tears away. "Oh! Metaphors—yes. What would we do without them? We'd have to get real."

"Metaphors are real, Hannah." Sarah didn't look at her.

"You and Wyatt! Metaphor mongers! Simile specialists! Yes, well." She glanced at the front door. "I hope Wyatt found shit with that fat guru. Fine for him to flit among the clouds pretending he doesn't have an ego, but he bloody better leave you here with me."

Sarah smiled at her cigarette, but she looked sad. Tired. Whoever Wyatt was and whatever this was about, it was apparently old ground.

Behind Hannah, a voice offered a shy, "Right on cue."

A thin blond man entered. He looked about fifty, with

intelligent blue eyes and a stooped, timid air. He wore worn corduroy, jeans and jacket.

Hannah dropped her cigarette into an ashtray, stood there staring.

Sarah smiled, very slowly.

The man straightened, his smile matching hers as it creased the skin around his eyes.

Hannah said, "You bastard! Oh!"

He turned his smile on her. It grew progressively more sheepish as he approached her. They stood face-to-face for a moment before she laughed her little-girl laugh and threw her arms around him. I was surprised to see his hands wander past her waist and down along her hips.

Hannah repeated, "Bastard!"

When Sarah stood, the man crossed to her. She extended both hands and he held them. I wondered if I'd ever seen two people look happier to see each other.

"It was good," he said. "Really good, Sarah."

She nodded. "Of course it was."

Hannah said sharply, "No, no, don't you start. I insist on five minutes of absolute quotidian nothing small talk before you start. Five minutes of 'Hello, how are you?' before you deluge us in guru talk!"

"Did you hear what the Buddhist said to the hot dog vendor?" The man grinned, glancing from her to Sarah. " 'Make me one with everything.' " Without waiting for a laugh, he looked at me and observed, "You have company." He sounded mildly surprised.

"You catch us *in medias res*."

"For once."

Sarah explained. "Karen's people sent them. To ask us questions."

The man folded her into his arms. It was a loving embrace, but his hands did not wander. "Will Karen's people—"

"Hear us?" she finished for him. "No. They don't know how."

He shifted so that he had one arm around her. "They couldn't come here themselves." He shook his head. It wasn't a question.

"You knew Karen?" Sandy hazarded.

"I'm Ted's father." He continued holding McGuin's mother tightly to him, but his eyes drank in Hannah Arthur. Then he focused on us. "I've been away thirteen months."

"Where 'bouts?" Sandy's question seemed casual, purely conversational.

"With my guru." He glanced at Sarah. "Jumping into the flame."

She smiled up at him. "Realizing you've always been in the flame."

His laugh was somewhere between a quiet giggle and a chuckle.

Hannah Arthur said, "Oh! Don't you even start quoting that fat old fart! You must be through with him by now?"

"His teachings have carried me far enough to go farther."

Hannah snorted.

Sarah seemed pleased. "That's exactly how it should be, Wyatt."

"I run in bigger and bigger circles to get where you are."

"I'm going to be sick!" Hannah informed them. "No Hallmark Zen guru commune claptrap . . ." Words seemed to fail her. She groped in her pockets, pulling out a crumpled pack of cigarettes.

"So I've been traveling," the man concluded. He offered Sandy his hand. "Wyatt Lehommedieu."

"You've all got different last names," Sandy observed.

"Arthur is Hannah's ex-husband's name," Sarah offered. "I kept our family name even though I'm married to Wyatt, and Ted has the last name Wyatt was born with."

"I changed mine legally six years ago," Wyatt explained.

"Lahomma . . . homma do?"

"That's right: Luh homma do. It's French—it means man of god, or man-god, depending on how literally you translate it."

"You, um, chose the name? Not a family name?"

"I chose it." He looked proud of having done so. "That and Wyatt. I was not a John."

"You chose not to be," Sarah said.

"Huh!" Hannah scoffed. "You forced us all to pretend you weren't!"

"A name is a defining thing. I don't know why you can't respect me enough to take this seriously."

"She takes it seriously," Sarah said patiently. "You know that."

Lehommedieu said, "Do you want me to leave for a while while you talk?"

Sandy shook his head. "Very useful to have you here. Karen's family just wants details. Insight. They're in a pretty bad way, you can imagine."

"Yes. Okay." He kissed Sarah's smooth brown cheek. "Is Teddy coming?"

"What do you think? He hasn't had a decent chess game in a year."

Hannah added, "We sold the batik and velvet angel. So we have caviar. And port." When she smiled, she looked incapable of ire. She looked like a happy kid.

Wyatt grinned back. A moment of eye contact made her smile fade, put that impossible ire back in her face. Sarah patted Wyatt's hand.

"So." Sandy shifted uncomfortably on his long legs. "We were wondering what you could tell us about Karen. If you saw any of this coming."

"No!" Hannah shook her head emphatically.

Sarah sighed. "Yes. We did. I suppose we did."

Hannah lit her cigarette with shaking fingers. "All that sparkle and up-so-floating."

" 'Many bells down.' " Sarah quoted e.e. cummings sadly. "Karen did sparkle and float around us. She was very switched on, very warm. Surfacely happy. Around us."

"Like Ted," Hannah interjected. "But not quite. Ted can be absolutely larger than life."

"What did you used to call him? A one-man play?" Wyatt smiled.

"That's what Karen loved about him," Sarah agreed. "His *here*ness, the way he'd fill up the stage. It pours out of him. Whereas with Karen—well, all that shine was on top, she'd just pull it over herself. To make us happy, I think. Because we'd feel so tarnished sometimes. So dark."

"Huh! You speak for yourself, Sarah. We're the goddamn new pennies! We're the goddamn Christmas tree lights!"

"The hard thing"—Sarah's soft voice grew smaller—"we knew all the time that she was cowering under her own charm. Part of why we responded to it was that it seemed so brave and transparent. But there was no way to make her believe we loved what was underneath, too. That we loved the outside because it came from what was inside. That we loved her right through."

"Oh!" This time Hannah's cry was pure distress. She clapped a hand over her eyes and turned away. "All that pain," she said.

Sarah turned into Wyatt's arms, burying her face. Her shoulders began to shake.

Wyatt nodded. "She was fun. She could click into that crazy Teddy space. But our feeling for her was . . ."

"Unconditional," Hannah said.

Sarah's voice was muffled. "She didn't believe in unconditional."

Wyatt wrapped his arms more tightly around her. His face scrunched and he too began to cry.

"Wyatt," Hannah whispered. She joined them, their arms accommodating a third as if from long practice.

Hannah murmured, "Yes, yes, we have caviar and port. And we'll call Teddy and he'll fly to us. And we will be utterly blind and utterly ourselves and have a wonderful evening. And I will have no guru talk for the next half hour, do you hear me? Wyatt? Sarah?"

Sarah broke away and hurried from the room, her face streaked with tears.

Hannah straightened her spine, fixing us with a look of great dignity. "We simply cannot say any more to you now. I hope that you will take this terrible reality away with you before we flay ourselves to death with it."

I moved closer to Sandy, slipping my arm through his. I felt weak, needed to touch someone.

"Yes ma'am," Sandy said. "We appreciate the time you gave us. Appreciate it much."

"Your wall hangings are beautiful," I blurted again.

And again, Hannah Arthur showed no sign of caring what I thought.

8

A HALF HOUR later, Karen Clausen's mother opened the door to us. Behind her, a gold velvet couch and heavy glass coffee tables relieved the gloom of closed curtains. The smell of fried chicken hovered like a greasy cloud. Two men sat in Herculon recliners, their eyes glued to a noisy ball game, its din punctuated by the sound of a ball being bounced against some outside wall. One man was overweight and balding. The other was younger and slimmer, with curlier, more abundant hair. Otherwise they looked alike: tall and florid in dark polo shirts, slacks, and generic running shoes. They hardly glanced at us. For the duration of the ball game, maybe always, the wife took care of everyday matters.

She reminded me of my mother, what my mother might have looked like now. (What I might look like, one day.) Her black hair was sprayed into an Ann Landers helmet, her skin was as smooth as china, her eyes were green and puffy-lidded, her nose large, her lips full and dark even without lipstick. Her face looked late fortyish but she carried another decade on her hips. With her navy-blue shift and white wedgie slippers, she looked like an Italian housewife circa 1959.

Which was the last year anyone was able to photograph my second-generation Italian mother.

The first thing she said was, "We're Catholic."

Sandy didn't skip a beat. "I'm Sander Arkelett from White, Sayres and Speck. Remember me, Mrs. Clausen? The investigator? And this is Ms. Di Palma. She's an attorney."

"My goodness. Of course it's you." The woman flushed, looking over her shoulder at the seated men. The younger one rose. "I wasn't—I thought you were Jehovah's Witnesses. They're always couples."

Before she finished speaking, the young man had elbowed her aside to stand in front of her. I couldn't tell if the gesture was protective or dismissive.

"I hope we haven't come at an inconvenient time."

The woman snapped, "You could forget that damn game for a minute and come talk to these people, Jerry! It's the lawyers. About Karen."

The man on the recliner glanced away from the television, then back, then away again. "Huh?"

"The lawyers from San Francisco." She took a step toward him, out of her son's shadow. Her nostrils flared. "For God sake."

"Ma." The son's tone said, Mellow out.

"You've been in that chair since lunchtime! All you do is sit in that chair! You can't even get up to talk about Karen."

"Ma."

The man rose reluctantly, half his attention still on the play in progress. "Invite them in, Clara. You don't need me to do that."

The young man displayed no emotion. Maybe he was used to their bickering. Maybe the interlude since his sister's death had been one of constant stress; maybe it just didn't register anymore.

The woman who looked like my mother flew across the room. "It's the lawyers!" Her tone verged on hysterical as she hit the mute button of the remote control.

"So invite them in and I'll get some beers. Jesus!"

Sandy entered the house, forcing the son to step back. "I could use a beer, thanks."

I followed. "None for me."

The man, his gaze wandering again to the television, received a verbal slap from his wife: "You heard him, Jerry! Get a beer!"

Two sweaty boys slouched through a door apparently leading to the kitchen. They were about twelve, dressed in shorts and soccer shirts, their hair matted with sweat and their faces shiny. Each slurped a canned soft drink.

"Almost dinnertime. Put those back," the young man commanded.

The darker-haired of the two boys complained, "When do we eat? I'm hungry."

Karen's mother swooped down on him, covering his sweaty face with kisses. "Got your favorite. Your very most favorite fried chicken and potato salad. You can drink that drink, but no more till after dinner, okay?"

The boy didn't pull back. He presented accommodating cheeks to be kissed. The other boy looked away, clearly embarrassed.

"That's my son William. And his friend Gene. I'm Mark Clausen, Karen's brother."

Sandy shook the man's hand. "Hope we're not interfering with your dinner."

"No, no," Mrs. Clausen cried. "Join us."

I had a feeling Sandy was about to accept, so I said, "I'm sorry. We only have a few minutes." This wasn't my project. I had no intention of sitting through dinner with Ozzie and his premenstrual Harriet.

"Can we eat now? Do we have to wait?" William's tone was peevish.

"Go back outside," the boy's father commanded. "You'll eat when Ricky gets his butt—"

"You help yourself, sweetheart," the boy's grandmother contradicted. "Salad's in the refrigerator, and the chicken's—"

"They can wait till Ricky gets here, Ma. That damn kid—"

"You leave Ricky alone! Why should William wait for his brother?"

"You've got the table set. Damn kid—he'll be here or I'll tan his—"

"Stop with Ricky! 'The table set'! It doesn't matter." She bent closer to her grandson, cooing instructions into his ear. He continued drinking his soda.

Mark Clausen was tight-lipped, hitting his son with a hot-eyed, nonverbal warning.

Seeing it, Jerry Clausen said, "The boys can wait ten more minutes, Clara."

She straightened. "Why?—tell me that. Why should they? Who did all the work? Me, that's who. If I say it's okay they eat now, why shouldn't they?"

"Their father—"

"I let *him* eat when he wanted." She turned a smoldering, resentful face to her son. "Didn't you always eat when you wanted?"

"Ma! You know Ricky's going to—"

"Jesus Canary." Jerry Clausen walked wearily across the room. "Beer coming up."

"Martyr! My God, I ask him to do one thing! After I've been cooking for him all day!"

"Ma."

"You boys go now and get some chicken. You can eat on the patio." She planted a few more loud kisses on her grandson's cheek.

By the time her husband returned with the beer, Mark had offered us the couch.

We all sat. There was a moment of awkward silence while Sandy sipped beer.

I waited for him to say something. He didn't. Just sipped, glancing at me.

Transparent bastard, wanting to get me back into the game. As if dilettanting around with this case would recommit me to the glorious practice of law.

Nevertheless, I obliged him. If I screwed it up for him, all the better, damn him. "We just came from your son-in-law's parents' house," I informed them.

Silence. The father glowered at the TV screen. The mother stared at me, her eyes wide and her jaw obviously clamped. Only the son moved: he squirmed slightly in his recliner.

"They're artists, I gather." I reminded myself that the Clausens were in mourning, that this must be excruciating for them. Damn Sandy anyway, leaving me to twist in the wind. "They seemed very fond of Karen."

The mother detonated. "Fond? Fond? Those cheap people, those hippies? They didn't know our Karen at all. They're users, that's what they are. Don't you be fooled! They were fond of Karen's money and how much she helped them. They're nothing but parasites. Imposing on her innocence!" Her eyes filled with tears. "Him too. We tried a million times to tell her."

Eyes still fixed on the television, the father said, "That son of a bitch." He blinked rapidly.

"She was a happy girl, a nice girl. She was going to go back to school and become a teacher before she met that hippie. So don't you talk to me about them being fond of her—"

"They're a bunch of bums." The father spoke to Sandy. "They don't work, half the time they're broke on their butts and supposedly he helps them out of his paycheck, but hell, it was Karen's money they were living on really. He empties his pocket and she's carrying him on her back. It was too damn much for her. We tried to tell her it's a sociological fact about . . . you know."

"Black men?" Sandy offered.

"You hear it all the time, all the studies. It's their women that support them. They don't mind admitting it. Hell, you can see from his family, they don't grow up with the value of hard work. They're trained from an early age to be users."

Mark Clausen rubbed his eyes. I hoped this was hard for him to listen to. I hoped his parents' beliefs were generational.

"Let me show you pictures. Where's the album, Jerry?"

"She was a beautiful girl," Jerry emphasized. "We couldn't get her to try out for homecoming queen or anything like that because, you know, they just weren't doing that in the early seventies, but she always liked nice clothes and, and . . . my brother's a lawyer in Seattle, he always said how refined she was. That's just how she was. Honor roll, smart. Pretty."

"She was going to go back to school and become a teacher," the mother repeated.

The father slumped. "She loved kids when she was young. We always thought she'd get married and have a family."

"I'm sure *he* didn't want children. They're selfish people. 'Artists'! That means me-me-me."

"Just as well they didn't have children."

I turned to Mark. "Was Karen a younger sister?"

"Five years younger."

"Were you close?"

He shrugged.

"What was she like? Speaking as a contemporary."

"She was good to the kids—brought them things when she went on vacation. Good to Ricky. She'd take him out on that little dinghy—"

"I told her it's too dangerous!" Clara Clausen sat straight with anger.

"How was I supposed to stop them?" Mark's tone was defensive. "She was no better than Ricky when it came to advice, you know that. And it's not like I've got time to take him boating and hiking and all that. Even if he *wanted* to spend time with me."

From the front of the house came the high squeak of bicycle tires on pavement.

Mark Clausen leaped to his feet. "God damn that kid!"

"You leave him alone," his mother said absentmindedly.

"Look at that! Six-thirty!" A few long strides carried Mark to the front door. He flung it open, shouting, "You know how to tell time, goddamn it? You know what five o'clock means? I was getting ready to drive around looking for you! After the damn embarrassment last month, calling the cops, and you waltz in in the middle of the night—"

I heard a sullen voice. Didn't quite catch the words.

"Get in here! If you're late again, that's it. I'll sell that damn bike, swear to God!"

"You shut up, Mark." Again Clara Clausen spoke without heat. "He's fifteen. You don't remember what you were like at fifteen?"

A gangly boy, red-faced with exertion and damp with sweat, entered the house. He slipped past his father.

"Sweetie pie. My big boy." His grandmother raised her

arms, compelling him to bend into her embrace. Then she ruffled his dark hair, saying, "My oldest grandson, Ricky."

The boy watched me and Sandy, his eyes narrowed and his head hanging.

"Go wash up, goddamnit." His father slammed the front door. "You think we like waiting for you all afternoon?"

"Let him alone! I suppose you cooked the dinner? If I don't care, why should you care?" She offered her cheek to Ricky, but he didn't kiss it.

He glowered at his father, his lips pinched and his shoulders hunched. He left the room in jerky haste, the stench of his exertion lingering.

Sandy waited a polite minute. "You were saying about Karen?"

"Beautiful girl," Jerry Clausen murmured. He stared at the muted television, eyes glazed with tears.

Beautiful girl, honor roll, good aunt. We didn't need the woman's stats, we needed some glimpse of her personality. We needed their version of what McGuin's family had provided.

But maybe the Clausens hadn't known their daughter. Maybe they hadn't seen past the stats. Plenty of that in my family, God knew.

"You say your name's Di Palma?" Clausen asked hesitantly.

"Yes."

"Related to the mayor?"

"He and my father are second cousins."

He broke into a wide grin. "Well, we're good buddies, me and Henry. You tell him you talked to Jerry Clausen, will you? Tell him hey."

"I will." He seemed to want me to say more; kept grinning like we were friends now too.

Clara Clausen took me off the hook. "Those McGuins are as much to blame— The way they sweet-talked and fussed. Users! That's all they are! Nobody likes to feel used!"

"I don't know, Ma. They—"

"That's what drove her crazy! People making you feel like they love you and all they want is to get something from you. Use you. She was like their little slave, going there and sewing for them and being their salesgirl at crafts fairs. Spending God knows how much money on them.''

Jerry Clausen nodded emphatically. "We warned her. People like that are two-faced. You can't trust them. They'll suck you dry.''

William Clausen erupted into the room. ''Grandma, where's dessert?'' he demanded.

"That's no way to ask," his father nagged.

"Leave him alone, Mark, he's just a boy." She rose, wiping away sudden tears. "Come on, sweetie, I'll show you. Maybe you can whip the cream for us.''

"I don't want to.''

"William!''

"Now just stop,'' Clara warned Mark. "Granny will do it.''

Jerry Clausen checked his wristwatch.

That seemed to be our cue. At any rate, I'd had more than enough.

"We should be going.'' I made sure my tone said, Right fucking now.

I had zero tolerance for family gatherings. Sandy knew that. Having met Hal's mother, my family matriarch, he also knew why.

"You go on ahead, Laura,'' Sandy drawled. "I think if these folks don't mind, I would truly love to try some of that fried chicken.''

For a surprised instant the family was silent. Then Clara Clausen said, "That would be nice. We have plenty.''

He dug his keys out of his pocket. "Call you later for a ride?''

I nodded, wondering if I'd let him down. Of course there was more to be learned from the family: picture albums to be viewed, chronologies to construct, anecdotes to ponder. But that wasn't my job; I didn't work for Steve Sayres.

I took the rental car keys, glad to be walking away from other people's problems with no obligation to analyze or compromise or litigate them away. No obligation to pump harder, think deeper, be tougher.

I'd have to make Sandy understand: adrenaline wasn't my drug anymore.

9

THERE WERE THREE cars in the driveway I'd ordered constructed the first time my tires got stuck in mud. Behind my little Mercedes was a rusting Honda I didn't recognize. Beside it was a flashy new Chrysler: Hal's mother's car.

I considered turning around and leaving. I had no reason to love the woman who'd imperiously stepped in for my deceased mother every time I wanted to do anything she considered déclassé. By virtue of her marriage to my "uncle" Henry, "aunt" Diana had asserted her right to thwart even my tamest adventures. My father was of a generation disposed to leave social matters to women, and he'd let this woman pen me and harass me until I'd eloped to be free of her. To this day, Papa remained baffled by my lack of gratitude for Diana's "feminine intervention" (even he couldn't call it motherliness). But for all her martyred bragging that she'd raised me, her only tangible contributions had been occasional bakery sweets and a weekly list of instructions for the housekeeper.

Even if I forgave Diana's (no way I'd call her aunt anymore) treatment of me, I'd never forgive her treatment of Hal. She'd seen her son as a mere accessory, praising him when he fit her shallow image, haranguing him when he drew attention to its flaws. She didn't even tell us he was wounded in Vietnam: the wound was inflicted by Hal's Vietnamese lover—a yellow person—and the story, she felt, did not reflect well on the family. I couldn't imagine why Hal—who'd stayed away from her years at a time—didn't wash his hands of her now, in the middle of the sideshow she'd made of her "utterly devastating" divorce. He'd turned away when she'd hurt him; why turn back because she was hurt? Why not let her fry in her own acid?

Damn.

I climbed reluctantly out of Sandy's rented Nissan. I knew Hal needed rescuing, knew his mother locked him into no-win confrontation with his own anger.

I pushed the front door open, expecting to see Diana in her usual overdressed splendor, drawling rotten things about my uncle. Her friends were sick of the carnage, and my father had escaped to Italy for the summer. Hal and I were the only spectators left in the arena.

I was surprised to find Diana sitting in pinch-lipped, wide-eyed silence on my sofa. With her Margaret Thatcher coif and chinless overbite, she looked braced and affronted.

The apparent reason for her reticence was Ted McGuin, chest out, arms slightly back, and chin tilted up; very much in Hal's face.

Hal looked shut down, stone-faced—the usual result of spending time with his mother. Either McGuin's ire was insufficient to snap him out of it, or it had the effect of clamping the emotional lid more tightly.

I tossed the Hertz keys onto the entryway table. I needed a quick Stoli.

"Hi," I said. "Can I get anyone a drink?"

McGuin turned. His wide brows met, dipped, straightened over eyes that all but crackled. The combination of brooding aggression and boiling stillness seemed almost telekinetic.

The angle of his head, the expression on his face changed suddenly, for all the world as if he'd caught my thought and been surprised by it.

"Drink, anyone?" I repeated. I crossed to the cabinet where I kept glasses and alcohol.

"McGuin thinks I tried to kill him today," Hal said flatly.

I glanced at him. He looked and sounded weary. McGuin's doing or his mother's?

"This is outrageous," Diana quavered. "Good Lord!"

"He thinks I messed with his diving equipment while you guys were in the house talking," Hal continued.

I poured myself the drink. "How exactly?"

McGuin's head was cocked. He watched me as he might watch an alien creature, something utterly outside his experience: some languid Noël Coward heroine, tossing back her cocktail.

"Do you dive?" McGuin's voice matched his stance: taking no shit.

"No."

"There's a valve you turn to let air out of your tank and into the part that goes into your mouth—the regulator. I was on my way down to the water when you came over. I had the valve open all the way so air would flow out if I sucked on the regulator. I didn't check it again when you left. Not till it stopped giving me air twenty feet underwater."

"What was wrong with it?"

"The valve was turned back for minimal air flow. Enough to get me down relatively deep. Then it was like trying to suck air out of a rock."

"Can't you turn the valve underwater? Increase the air flow?"

Hal spoke. "He says it was superglued."

"I thought it was just stuck. I don't know what the fuck I thought, except that I needed to get my ass back up to the surface." He shot an angry glance at Hal. "I could have been in serious trouble. If I'd been diving deep."

"When he came up and checked it, he saw it was glued."

"Fucking thing's ruined." McGuin slid a quick hand over his curls. "I have a spare, but fuck." He took a few steps to the sofa and dropped down beside Diana. Both looked shaken.

"Why would Hal do that?" I wondered.

"I was alone with the equipment."

I was having trouble reading Hal. Why so much distance? Because he disliked McGuin and didn't regret the near drowning? He never was good at feigning sympathy.

"This is slander!" Diana piped. "I don't know who you are or why you—"

"Goodness, Hal, you didn't introduce them? Ted McGuin, Diana Di Palma."

"McGuin," Diana repeated. "You're the man who . . . did that to his wife."

McGuin shot her a glance so cold anyone else would have been affected by it.

"His wife killed herself," I corrected.

"But he . . ." Manners won out over scandal, and she left the sentence hanging.

"You're saying you didn't do it." McGuin considered Hal.

"Even if I walked around with superglue in my pocket—"

"There was a tube in my toolbox five feet from the regulator," McGuin interrupted. "Do you know scuba equipment?"

Hal crossed his arms over his chest, leaning back against the plank wall.

I watched him, feeling a tingle of apprehension. I had no idea whether he knew how to scuba dive. It seemed, lately, there was much I didn't know about him. I didn't know he'd come back to Hillsdale to see McGuin's wife.

I took a fast swallow of Stoli. Either I was too self-centered to explore Hal's history or he was too taciturn to allow it. Probably both.

After four years together it made me feel like the relationship was hollow. Only as deep as our physical, maybe our familial connection.

I looked at Hal and thought, I love you, but we're not friends.

I said, "Do you know how to scuba dive, Hal?"

He glanced at me, a tiny smile on his face. "Yes, Mowgli, I do."

Mowgli. He hadn't called me that in years. But then, it had been years since I'd allowed my hair to justify the nickname.

"Since high school." Diana's tone said, Surely you remember, Laura? "I could not stop him."

I was sure she'd done her best. And with her connections, her best could be formidable.

I turned to McGuin. "You're out of line. Accusing Hal is just plain silly. You don't have any reason to think he means you harm."

It surprised me McGuin wasn't at the Clausen house accusing them. They'd be damn glad to see him drown.

But maybe he couldn't face them. Maybe it was easier to attribute homicidal animosity to Hal, a relative stranger.

"I stayed inside five minutes after you left," McGuin said carefully.

"Then that's the five minutes someone glued your valve."

McGuin sat back, causing Diana to move fastidiously deeper into her corner.

"It's so unreal it's hard to think about." McGuin's wince underscored his words. "But if I don't think about it, if it stops mattering to me, then that's fucked too."

I wasn't quite sure I followed. Apparently Hal did. He said, "It's less trouble. Take my word for it."

"No." McGuin bounded to his feet. "That's a dangerous attitude. Self-destructive."

Hal shook his head wanly. "It's reality. Going with the flow."

"Getting fucking flowed over. And being too—I don't know—cowardly to stand up and buck the tide."

They locked eyes. Probably both men were wrong. But McGuin put more energy into it.

I liked that. Or maybe it just made a nice change.

10

I PICKED UP Sandy a short time later—time enough, unfortunately, to endure slanted details of Uncle Henry's settlement offer to Diana. I felt like driving to the house my uncle shared with my father and calling him a damn fool. The offer infuriating Diana was, in any lawyer's opinion, far too generous. She wouldn't be satisfied with anything less than his genitals anyway; why not be sensible? A man of my uncle's generation and background would feel guilty no matter what. Why translate that into pauperizing reparations? If anyone was at fault, it was Diana, not Henry. She'd driven their only son away, depriving the family of the truth and making it accomplice to her cruelty. More than once I'd hit Uncle Henry with my distillation of legal advice and family feeling: Screw her. He wouldn't listen, and I couldn't help that.

Nor could I help it if Papa considered my view cold and uncharitable. My emotions were safe from Diana's manipulation; his weren't.

Sandy was waiting for me outside the Clausens' ranch-style bungalow. It was in a well-to-do neighborhood of large sixties tract houses with showcase garages. Sandy was pacing up the block, glancing into neighbors' side yards, upsetting their dogs. Force of habit, I supposed.

"Hi." He slid into the seat beside me, fondly patting the Mercedes leather. "Thanks for picking me up."

"I wish I'd stayed with you. Diana's over."

"Mmm."

"McGuin came by too."

"Yuh?"

"Someone glued the valve of his scuba tank so he'd run out of air underwater." I added, "He says."

I took my eyes off the wide, untrafficked street to monitor his reaction.

Sandy raised his pale brows. "Why come to you?"

"Ostensibly to accuse Hal. Because Hal was alone with the equipment for a while."

We drove in silence over a roller-coaster hill flanked by dripping gullies. I didn't have to ask Sandy what he thought. At this point he'd be compiling questions. I was too. When it came time to hazard a conjecture, one of us would speak. We'd done this before.

"Avoidance," I finally offered. "He's not going to put himself through a session with the Clausens, even if they're obviously the ones to accuse."

"But he's too mad to sit home and keep his mouth shut."

"He knows Hal didn't do it. It was pure bluster. The minute I called him on it, he deflated."

Sandy nodded. "Question is, did it really happen?"

"Do you want to go by there? Talk to him? I'm up for it." Not up for the continuing melodrama of my "discarded" aunt.

"Sounds good." He slid a long-fingered hand over my knee. Quickly removed it. "Could have to do with you."

"What could?"

"Could be McGuin wanted to see you again."

A flattering assessment of my charms. Especially from a man who'd watched many witnesses and deponents take a strong dislike to me. "Could be he wanted to see Hal again."

"Someone to talk to about Karen? He could do that with his family."

"Maybe it's uncomfortable—can't say anything negative about her. They liked her too much."

"So did Hal."

We swung onto a highway rattling with logging trucks. Fine twists of redwood bark hit my windshield. The sky was beginning to glow twilight gold behind a high overcast.

"Well." Sandy drew the word out wearily. It must have been a long, trying dinner. "McGuin doesn't show it—he's too defensive—but you know he's got to feel like shit on some level."

"Ted Bundy didn't."

"I don't see McGuin as a sociopath, do you?"

"No," I admitted. "But he's got that martyred 'You don't know the whole story' air."

"And you're thinking, So did Wally Bean."

My most notorious client, assassin of two conservative senators, had tried to cultivate an air of mystery, of allegiance to historic and noble forces. In reality, Bean had been merely silly in his delusions.

"Maybe McGuin's pulling it off because he's smarter than Wally."

"Keep your eyes on the road? Yuh, I think it's a possibility. All that 'I don't owe you an explanation' bullshit—could be he doesn't have one. That it was just too hard living with a crazy, ugly lady."

"And he's romanticizing to make himself the misunderstood one."

"Yuh. Or it could have happened some way we don't get yet."

"No help from her family?"

"Mostly a lot of greasy chicken." Another sigh. "A lot of sad pictures. Girl looks like she wants to erupt right out of the family portrait, know what I mean?"

"Well, she did do that. Marrying a black man—"

"Who looks white."

"You said she left town for a while. Where'd she go?"

"San Francisco. Lived in the avenues. Went to school. Stopped about eight units shy of a teaching credential. Worked at Woolworth's, then at a bakery. Came home but wouldn't live with the parents. Rented for a while; then they helped her out with the down payment for the place you saw in Dungeness. She diddled a bit at the junior college—met McGuin when he was doing his medical tech course."

"No history of depression?"

"No public health record, not before the suicide attempt. Could be she went to someone private. Clausens say no. But I doubt they'd recognize depression, tell the truth."

"They wouldn't," I agreed. "Not if it reflected badly on them."

"McGuin moved out here from Colorado. Started at the state college, dropped out, worked loading trucks and got himself into the longshoremen's union. Moved his family out. Went to the junior college and got himself a medical tech certificate."

"She help him financially?"

"Must have, day to day. Part of his paycheck's been going to his family—their bank records show deposits on his paydays. And the IRS has been deducting for back taxes. Which wouldn't leave him much to help with household bills. And he's got some old debts hanging over him. Small-time consumer stuff, still owes money to the state college. Three, four grand, total."

Sandy always did his homework, always followed the paper trail before interviews.

"Laura?"

"Yes?"

"You've got to be bored up here. What are you doing?" It might have been an obnoxious personal question. But his tone said, I miss you. Come back.

We were past the main drag now, past the dying downtown of five-and-dimes and unstylish clothing stores. We followed a long curve of sporting goods stores, car washes, and blue-collar bars. In the first blush of twilight, they winked their fifties neon.

"Is Hal keeping you up here? Because you know my opinion on that—he's a hell of a lot more resilient than you give him credit for. He should be following you, not vice versa. You should be pulling him up instead of him dragging you down."

"I told you, Sandy: I needed a break."

"Sure, it was too bad what happened." White firing me, then having a heart attack as an indirect result. "But it's no use you taking it personally."

"It was personal."

"No it wasn't. It was just White being fiscal, you know what I mean. You were a cornerstone of that operation; they're hurting without you. It seems like you and Steve Sayres are cutting off your own noses."

"When I do go back to work, it won't be for Sayres. Guaranteed."

"When are you going back?"

"When it feels right."

" 'Cause if you're waiting for Di Palma to get his shit together—"

"No. He doesn't worry about that. He just . . . endures, I guess."

"That's screwed."

Sandy didn't understand the extent of Hal's problems.

"Some people go with the flow because that's the bravest thing they can do."

"Yes and no, Laura. If we're talking a blind man in a crowd, sure thing. If we're talking—"

"A disabled veteran, basically."

"No way!" Sandy's voice bordered on anger. "His worst problems are self-inflicted, and you're too smart to believe anything different."

I concentrated on the road. To our left, muddy wetlands mirrored the sky. To our right, evergreens shagged a hilly horizon.

We'd had some variant of this discussion a dozen times over the last four years. I was sick of trying to explain Hal, sick of trying to defend my relationship with him.

Or maybe I was less certain that I could; less convinced that I should.

"We're close."

"You're family."

"I love him."

"Family," he repeated.

"He's complicated, Sandy. Layered."

"You getting under any of those layers?"

We sped past blowing dune grass and piles of driftwood on an untrodden beach. Condensation beaded the Mercedes's windshield.

"Laura, listen: You're smart and slick and you know how to set your sights. That's healthy. I know Crosetti"—my last client, dead now—''got you thinking it was a shallow way to live. But remember who he came to when he was in trouble. He didn't go to his do-gooder friends, he came to you. And even if you want to beat yourself up about being a fancy lawyer, doesn't mean you should romanticize somebody never accomplished a damn thing in his life. 'Layered'—Di Palma's got himself bottled up so tight— He's a black hole, so tight he's pulling you in with him. You're imploding into him.'' I felt his hand on my knee. ''He might not give a shit, but I do.''

I ignored his hand and continued driving.

''Was a time you could have discussed this with me, you know that, Laura? Was a time you had the vocabulary.''

I'd never been much of a relationship analyzer, never disposed to intensive inner search. But he was right, I'd have been able to agree or disagree, at least.

''I'm not romanticizing, Sandy: Hal's complicated. He's been hurt. To the point where it's valiant he can keep quiet about it.''

''No. You're accepting his premise, and that's crap. Valiant is you deal with the problem.''

''I can wait till he's ready.''

''That might never happen.'' His hand tightened on my knee. ''And what do you get out of it meantime? Look where you are: your God damn hometown, which you put a lot of energy into outgrowing. Anybody makes you turn your back on what you've achieved, where you should be, that person's driving a hell of a hard bargain.''

I hit the accelerator, startled to hear Karen McGuin's phrase in this context. ''Look, I've spent most of my adult life keeping busy—achieving. But there's more to me than that.'' I hoped. ''I'm not what I've been doing.''

''Course you are. We all are.''

The wind whistled through seams in my convertible top. The air smelled of cold shore.

Five silent minutes later, we pulled onto McGuin's private road.

11

"**S**O WHERE IS he?" Sandy pounded on the front door again. Through sheer curtains, interior lights glowed. The smell of refried beans and garlic hung over the porch.

Sandy moseyed down the swollen, unpainted steps. He crunched through weedy gravel and laid his hand on the hood of McGuin's car. "Cold," he commented. "Been home awhile."

"Maybe he went for a walk."

"Or got picked up by somebody." He moved quickly around the car toward the steep footpath to the sea. To his left was a wooden shed, its double doors gaping open. Sandy stepped inside.

I left the porch, admiring the dull mauves of twilight, noticing—and being aware of noticing—shrubs along the path. Six months ago they'd have been vague masses of green to me. But Hal had taught me to differentiate hemlock, yarrow, cow parsnip; to appreciate Devonian relics like horsetails and ferns; to see individual plants in luxuriant jumbles of vine. I wondered if Sandy would find that as impressive as my knowledge of bankruptcy codes and UCC regulations.

"Well," Sandy called out, "his wet suit's in here. His

scuba stuff. But something's gone, something big. Something usually sits on padded cinder blocks. Little boat, maybe.''

I trailed after him, peering into the shed. It was a low-roofed rectangle, maybe ten by twenty feet, with a table saw and other tools set up on benches in the back, and scuba gear and a big empty space in front.

''I'd say a boat,'' Sandy continued. ''Padded blocks—maybe an inflatable. And up here—he'd have to carry it on down, so yeah, definitely an inflatable, I'd say.''

''You think he's using it now?''

''He left your place how long ago?''

It seemed like I'd been sitting forever, listening to my aunt complain; it seemed like five hours at least. ''Maybe two hours, hour and a half.''

''Yuh. He'd have time to paddle out a ways. Doesn't look like he's doing any diving, though, unless he's got more than one suit and tank. And I don't see any sign of an outboard engine—no rack, no gas can—so he's probably close to shore. You got on walking shoes?''

It showed how radically my life had changed that I could say, ''Of course.''

''Let's go down. See if he's close.''

I didn't care as much about McGuin as I did the walk. Growing up, I'd felt obliged to ignore my hometown's natural beauty; no use liking a place I was determined to leave. But now, having chosen to return, I could admire the drama of land and climate. I could apply it like balm to a frazzled psyche. I was frazzled now, after a day of Sandy's interviews; I was out of social shape.

I preceded Sandy along the path. To our right, Dungeness Head extended like a low, lush mountain perhaps a quarter mile out, creating a cove of flat sea. Gray rocks, some as big as cars, piled the bottom and stippled the shore. Smoothed by surf and tide pool plants, from a distance they resembled hunks of bread.

There was enough daylight to get us down and back, with a few minutes for a quick search of the beach. The wind had come up, a cold slap in the face. I watched the ocean, a deeper shade of burgundied gray than the sky.

"That's probably him out there. Small inflatable, going slow—he's rowing."

I scanned the sea. The minute my eyes found the boat—a yellow oblong the size of a discarded matchbook—it exploded in small torches of flame, one in front and one in back. From a distance they resembled flashes of a cigarette lighter, long and sudden, quickly dying into plumes of black smoke.

"What the fuck?" Sandy's voice was quiet with shock.

The yellow oval folded in the middle as we stood gaping. A figure bobbed in the water. By the time Sandy pushed past me, running and sliding down the brambled path, the figure was executing a slow, water-treading circle around the ragged shape.

I followed Sandy, adrenaline pumping, cheeks scalding. What the hell had I just seen?

McGuin—assuming it was him—suddenly began to swim, a fast and steady stroke. As we neared the end of the path, a beach ringed with rock came into view. McGuin was a long way out.

Sandy's feet hit sand before mine. I was right behind him over fifty feet of driftwood-littered beach, the rush of tide drowning out his panting if not mine.

By the time we reached the shore, McGuin was less than a third of the way in. Considering it had taken us maybe five minutes to dash down the weedy path, McGuin had another ten- or-fifteen minute swim ahead of him.

Sandy stopped short at the tide line, grabbing my shoulders as freezing water shocked my feet.

McGuin was making steady progress, but was still a long way off shore. Much farther than I could ever swim.

"I'm no good in the water," Sandy panted. "Got to wait till he's closer, see if he gets in trouble. You go back, get inside, call for help. He's going to be fucking frozen. If he makes it."

If he makes it.

I didn't discuss. I went.

I scrambled uphill as fast as I could, tore through McGuin's yard, yanked his door. It was unlocked. I muddied a tidily swept floor, racketing from corner to corner searching for the telephone.

I called 911. Told them a boat sank. A man was swimming, I hoped not drowning. Send someone, I begged. I told them where to find us. Told them I'd be waiting on the beach.

Getting back downhill should have been quicker. I kept falling. It was dark, only the smallest glow of daylight on the horizon. When I hit the beach, I could hardly see the open water, only the white streaks of surf. And what I saw there seemed to make no sense.

McGuin was close now, not fifty feet off shore. But instead of swimming the rest of the way in, getting himself onto dry land, he was swimming in slow circles maybe ten feet in diameter. Doing an odd sidestroke that kept his head facing center at all times.

I could hear Sandy shout to him, shout his name, insist he swim to shore.

The wind sliced through my sweaters, flogged me with damp strands of my hair. I could feel every frozen degree of ocean spray on my face.

"McGuin," I heard myself shout.

I stood beside Sandy, watching McGuin continue his slow, head-to-center circles.

"What's he doing?" I repeated it several times, frantic for Sandy to explain.

"McGuin, goddamn it! Here!" Sandy's hand suddenly fell from his lips. "Jesus."

McGuin was thrashing now, not more than thirty feet from us.

"Damn! Damn!" Sandy's voice was bewildered, angry.

Another "Damn!" found him wading slowly, shoulders hunched with cold, into the freezing tide. Then he was prone, swimming inexpertly over the surf toward the floundering figure.

I watched them bob together for a moment, watched Sandy pull McGuin with weak strokes, then stand and drag him closer to shore.

I ran toward them, the scene suddenly floodlit. It was so surreal I didn't stop to consider that it must be the help I'd called for, that firemen were shining searchlights from the hillside to the beach.

My attention was focused on Sandy, shaking almost convulsively, coughing and streaming water as he deposited McGuin in shallow surf.

McGuin was just lying there, eyes wide open, staring at me. His clothes were sodden and seawater ran off him in small cascades, but he didn't shiver. He lay very still in the foamy surf, looking up at me. With his thick neck and almond eyes, wet curls pasted to his forehead, he looked like a felled statue.

He spoke slowly. "Thing about a shark, it won't attack if you look it in the eye. Look it in the eye, it's not sure you're dinner—dinner thrashes, tries to swim away. Make eye contact and it tries to figure out what you are. It watches you, swims around you. Like you're dancing. Looking into each other's eyes. Every time you have your back to shore, you swim backward a little and it swims forward, keeping the circle tight. So your circles keep getting closer and closer to shore. And then, wham"—a weak smile—"the water's too shallow and it goes away. That's what I did." The searchlights bleached his face, made him look otherwordly, almost dead. "Reef shark."

Sandy was on his knees in the surf, his body jerking and his teeth chattering as he vomited seawater.

McGuin continued to lie still. He reached up and wrapped his hand around my wrist. His hand was almost as cold as the water.

"That's what I kept telling Karen," he said. "Look it in the eye. The minute you turn around, the minute you run, it decides you're food. You've got to look it in the eye." He rolled toward me, forehead against my thigh as I knelt. "Why couldn't she get it? I'd have given anything, a leg, anything, just to get her to believe that—just that one thing."

Suddenly three men were on top of us, pulling me up and out of the way, bending over McGuin with flashlights, speaking professional code as they lifted him onto what looked like a wooden surfboard with handholds. They moved him to dry sand, cut off his wet clothes and wrapped him in blankets. I heard one man ask McGuin over and over what his name was, if he knew where he was. McGuin rambled about the reef shark as another man helped Sandy out of the surf and out of his clothes.

I heard one of the men say "moderate hypothermia," and the words danced in my head as Sandy, still shivering violently, accepted blankets. They echoed all the way back up the hill as the men carried McGuin, blanketed and strapped to the multi-handled board.

We found an ambulance waiting, its floodlights pouring dazzling brightness on the overgrown yard. Two men hopped out, bending over McGuin a brief moment as they talked to the firemen. Then they opened the back door of the ambulance, setting the wooden board onto a cot and strapping it into place. They ordered Sandy to lie on a bench along the other ambulance wall, and they handed me blankets, telling me to climb in front and cover my wet legs.

And in a dizzying rush we were off, flashing red lights reflected in the windows of McGuin's house.

Looking over my shoulder into the rear of the ambulance, I saw a medic bent over McGuin. He reached a hand behind him. The driver pulled a plastic IV bag off the dashboard, handing it back. He explained over the din of the engine, "Vent warms it a bit."

The medic was speaking loudly. "Do you know what happened? Ted? Do you know what happened to you?"

The driver asked me, "Does he have any history of convulsions? Drug use? Allergies?"

"I don't know. We just met."

McGuin was saying, "Reef shark. I had to look it in the eye."

"Shark?" The medic turned to Sandy.

"No. I didn't see any shark."

The driver piped in, "Couldn't have been a reef shark—they're warm water."

"Something happened to his boat," Sandy continued. "Little inflatable dinghy, from the look of it. We saw a couple of flashes of light. Looked like something popped it, cherry bombs or something."

"How long was he in?"

"Twenty-five, I'd say. Thirty minutes tops."

"How about you?"

"Couple of minutes. He was doing okay till he got right almost to surf line, then he started swimming in circles." Sandy made a series of shuddering noises. "Fuck, that water's cold."

"Current comes straight down from Alaska," the driver said, almost proudly. "Doesn't get much colder."

I strained to see what the medic was doing in the brightly lighted back of the ambulance. In the front, it was dark but for the reflection of red lights on glinting bits of road and car windshields.

The medic had already inserted the IV line, taping it to McGuin's arm. Now he rechecked a line hooking McGuin to some type of monitor.

The driver asked me for details, and I said, "I don't know, I just looked out there and saw these two flashes of light, and then the shape of McGuin's boat changed—it capsized. He swam around it, then he swam for shore. By the time I got back down there after calling you, he was swimming in circles, like Sandy said."

Staticky voices came over one of four intercoms mounted over the front windshield. The driver ignored it. "Did you see a shark out there?"

"No. I think he's rambling. He said something about how you're supposed to swim in circles so you don't lose eye contact, because a shark will attack if you do." The heater, the blanket on my legs—I didn't know when I'd appreciated warmth more.

I heard McGuin mutter, "Cold."

The medic responded. "You're with us, huh?"

"Dave?" McGuin said weakly.

"Sure enough. You know what happened?"

"Boat."

"Yeah?"

"Cold. Hypo— . . ."

"—thermia. Don't worry, we know what to do." He chuckled. "Hospital workers are the worst. They watch everything you do—you take some precaution and they interpret it as they're dying."

"Cold," McGuin repeated. "I've been out of it."

I watched him try to move the arm with the IV.

"Hey now," the medic said. "You're strapped in, okay? You know you're not supposed to move."

"Blood in the extremities . . ."

"Is acidotic and very damn cold and you don't want it hitting your heart right now. Good boy." He fiddled with the monitor lead. "What can you tell us, Ted?"

"Out maybe third of a mile. Boat blew up. Don't get it. Inflatable—has two chambers. Saw one blow—don't know why. Other one should have stayed inflated." For the first time, he spoke like he was shivering.

"It blew too," I heard Sandy say. "We saw two blasts, one in front, one in back."

"Turkey," the driver muttered to a car that was not moving out of the way. He hit a button, and the siren was deafening. He turned it off the minute the car moved over.

"What were you doing out there?" Sandy asked, a detective first and foremost.

"Paddling, thinking. Cold—goddamn!"

"How'd you get your boat to pop like that?"

McGuin tried to sit up.

"Damn it," the medic said, restraining him. Then to Sandy: "What the hell?"

"Sorry."

I twisted in my seat, trying to look at Sandy, but he was directly behind me, shielded by a wall.

Did he really think McGuin sank his own boat? Knowing he had twenty-five minutes of freezing water between him and the shore?

McGuin was a strong swimmer, that was certain. And the swimming in circles, the seeming disorientation, that might have been for our benefit, to make the swim seem more of a feat, the incident more life-threatening.

I'd have given anything for a private moment with Sandy. Did he really think McGuin had staged it? Staged the gluing of his scuba tank too?

Sandy wasn't given to fanciful suspicions. If he was entertaining that possibility, there had to be a reason. There had to be something about McGuin, maybe something about his wife's suicide, that Sandy hadn't told me.

12

I SAT IN an alcove of vinyl benches and particle board end
tables. The hospital corridor smelled of old linoleum and
harsh disinfectant. I watched gurneys being wheeled, families embracing and weeping, figures in scrubs rushing, nurses
in white pants suits chatting. Fluorescent tubes washed the
color out of passing flesh, made everything else surreally
vivid. Now and then intercom voices summoned doctors.

God, I hated this place. I hated the memories it summoned: my mother frail and full of tubes, a bedside conversation with my ex-husband, Sandy rasping from a bullet in
the lungs. I hated the smell, the sadness, the dreary cheap-
ness of the furniture. Why would anyone want to work here?
Why would anyone want to witness pain and decay?

I wondered if working here had helped McGuin cope with
his wife's grisly wounds. Maybe they'd seemed common-
place to him, not the object of horror they'd have been to
someone else. But then, why give her a loaded gun, day after
day?

Sandy interrupted my tape loop of musing.

"Howdy."

He looked rumpled in clothes the hospital had hastily dried

for him. He carried a paper bag which presumably held his shoes, since he wore only rubber-bottomed hospital socks.

"You're okay?"

"Yuh."

"Will they let us see McGuin?"

"Nope. They say it's a slow process, getting someone warmed back up. They've got to watch him—something about the blood in his arms and legs actually being bad for the heart. Anyway"—he shrugged—"they'll keep him in emergency for a while, till he stabilizes. Then they'll take him to transitional care. Probably keep him through tomorrow afternoon."

"Did he say anything else about the boat?"

"Not really. Medical people's questions were just to see if he's alert and oriented—least that's how it seemed to me. Sheriff's investigator's been in and out, but McGuin says he doesn't remember anything except ending up in the water." Sandy shook his head. "His family's in with him now. The nurses are booting them out, give the deputy a little elbow room. I figure they'll come wait here. Thought we could get everybody some coffee."

Thought we could pump them for information. "Sure."

We sat in silence, Sandy close enough for me to feel the warmth of his arm beside mine. A few minutes later, Ted McGuin's father and aunt exploded into the corridor.

Hannah Arthur was stabbing the air with her cigarette, saying, "Oh. Up on that phony guru plane! I will not accept platitudes and false comfort—lobotomized reality!"

To which Wyatt Lehommedieu responded by wrapping his arms around her. "Remember the old joke, the guru's on the mountaintop talking to a pilgrim: 'I'll be glad to tell you everything I know, but you've got to stop saying "Bullshit!" after everything I say.' "

She pushed him away, brushing sudden tears out of her eyes. I heard the hiss of burning hair as her cigarette met a renegade tendril.

Then she noticed us. "Oh. You."

Sandy said, "Can I get you folks some coffee? Sodas or something?"

McGuin's mother appeared behind them. The lights gave

her skin a yellowish cast. Shoulders rounded, brows pinched, she looked tired and depressed.

The three of them watched us, just watched, not responding. My impression, perhaps mistaken, was that they were unused to company, unused to conversing with those outside the family circle. But it was an unusual situation, one to make any family value its privacy.

I decided to help Sandy out. "Something cold for me."

"What can I bring you folks? Cold drinks all around?"

McGuin's aunt made a sound like a quiet sputter, which it suited Sandy to take for assent. His quick glance told me to keep my ears open in his absence.

I scooted to the far end of a padded bench. Sarah Gowan watched me, pressed her lips together, then pushed past her sister and sat at the other end.

"You saw it happen," she said.

"Yes." I described what I'd seen.

"Bright flashes," she repeated without inflection.

"Oh. Have we endured our share of those!" Hannah touched fluttering fingers to her forehead. "Gunpowder. Firecrackers."

A grin lit Lehommedieu's face. "Ted almost blew our house up once when he was twelve. Put a hole through the basement—"

"And the rain gutters!"

"He poured gasoline into the rain gutter and lit it."

I must have looked shocked by Lehommedieu's pride. McGuin's aunt said, "Oh no, no—not on purpose. Mr. Wizard. Into everything. Kitchen cabinets emptied and big bubbling volcanoes in the sink." A peep of vicarious mischief in her eyes.

"Fire and water," Lehommedieu continued. "I'd love to see his astrological chart. How often do you see that kind of duality?"

Sarah Gowan spoke quietly, distractedly. "Not duality. Generality. A general fascination. With life. With places. With experimentation."

"So what do you think blew his boat up?" Were they confirming Sandy's not-quite-articulated suspicion?

She covered her mouth with her hand.

Lehommedieu watched her, clearly puzzled. He took a step toward her, glanced at me, paused.

I stood, moving to the other bench. Lehommedieu sat beside his wife. She allowed him to take her hand, but she didn't make eye contact.

"Sarah?" he said. "He's okay."

"For how long, John?" Stress made her use the name he'd mentioned shucking.

"What do you mean?"

"Oh!" McGuin's aunt lit another cigarette from the butt of the old one, spoke through clamped lips. "She means it didn't go down by itself, you, you guru-sniffer!"

He blinked at her, his pale lashes adding innocence to an expression of bewilderment. "He must have had some firecrackers on board or something."

Hannah looked ready to spring at him, but her sister extended a "Stop it" hand.

Sarah turned to face her husband, her brown eyes huge and liquid, her face a study of pinched seriousness. "This is not good, Wyatt." Her raspy smoker's voice lent emphasis to the words. "Of course he didn't have firecrackers on board. And if he did, he wouldn't have set them off near the rubber. You know how careful he is."

Sandy appeared behind Hannah then, his hands wrapped around a bouquet of paper cups. Small ice cubes tumbled from one.

Sarah looked at Hannah. "Do you understand?"

"Oh." A wide arc of her head sent more red hair spilling from its topknot. "Like it's not obvious!"

When she didn't continue, I prompted, "Obvious?"

"Oh, Hannah." Sarah sounded disappointed, almost exasperated.

I couldn't decide if she was shutting her sister up or telling her she was wrong.

"I missed a lot this year, didn't I?" Wyatt said simply.

"What else is new, buster?" Hannah paced a tight, angry circle that nearly launched her into Sandy's drinks.

Sandy said, "I hope you folks like Seven-Up. It's about all they've got besides machine coffee." I could hear regret in his voice; was surprised he hadn't hung back, listening for the scene to play out.

He handed around the drinks. McGuin's aunt was still now, arms wrapped around herself. The parents sat side by side, barely touching, staring at what appeared to be the same spot on the scrubbed linoleum.

Sandy waited for them to take a sip. "The sheriff's investigator wants to talk to me and Laura. Routine questions. I told him he could come do that here, if it's all right with you."

"No." Hannah Arthur dropped her cigarette into her drink and turned away.

"I suppose we could talk to him down the hall. Thought you might want to hear, though."

"Talk to him down the hall," Sarah said gently. "Please."

"We'll come back after and chat a minute." Sandy didn't pose it as a question; he knew what the answer would be.

I stood reluctantly, wanting inexplicably to remain with these people.

As I threaded past Sandy, he muttered, "Sheriff's got a fire under his tail, or I'd have waited a bit."

In fact, several yards down the hall, a plainclothes deputy glanced crabbily at his wristwatch.

Sandy was about to introduce us, when the deputy said, "Hell, we know each other."

He looked to be in his late thirties, with a thinning buzz cut and a full mustache. Judging from his posture and stance, he was fit as well as trim. He did look familiar, but not familiar enough for the smile that curled his lips.

"Remember me, kiddo? Jay Bartoli?"

I took a shocked step backward, spilling a bit of my drink. Jay Bartoli, to whom I'd run once—but only once—after learning of my husband's infidelity. Christ, almost twenty years ago. Jay Bartoli, whose father had helped mine keep the family books, advised him on investments, supplied us with endless fresh salmon during fishing season. Jay Bartoli, in whose freezing pool we'd had brave swimming parties. Bartoli, former peace activist and longhair, with whom I'd split my first decent ounce of grass.

I guess he followed my train of thought. "Well, you too," he said. "You're looking pretty straight, too."

I stepped into a quick embrace. We both laughed.

"I used to see Gleason around quite a bit." Gary Gleason, my ex-husband—just hearing the name caused bile to rise in my throat. "I guess you heard he moved away when his wife died. Up to Seattle, I heard."

Seattle—not nearly far enough.

Sandy, aware of my loathing and the reasons for it, artfully changed the subject. "I'm surprised you got someone over here so fast. You hear from the fire department? That it was sabotage?"

Bartoli continued smiling at me for a minute before turning his attention back to the matter at hand. "No. We got a call from McGuin late this afternoon stating someone tampered with his scuba equipment. We told him we'd send a deputy over tonight, around eight, eight-thirty. We must have just missed the excitement."

"You were late," Sandy observed.

"Yeah, well, it's not like he was in any danger of reusing the faulty equipment, you know? We didn't put a priority on it."

"I just meant if you'd been on time, you'd have seen it happen."

If McGuin had indeed staged the capsizing of his own boat, he'd waited for his audience. Only it was me and Sandy up on the hill looking down at him, not the sheriffs he'd expected.

"That's unfortunate," Bartoli agreed. "So let's hear about it. You got there around what time?" He extracted a small notebook from his sport jacket pocket.

We ran the scenario for him. It didn't take long. Shorn of scrambling and drama, there was surprisingly little to say.

"You think we could talk to you sometime about the wife? McGuin's wife? That case?" Sandy's voice was pleasant, unurgent.

Bartoli hesitated, then glanced at me. "I guess so—don't see why not. Stop by and I'll dig out the file for you." He leaned closer. "So, Laura, you're back in Hillsdale, huh?"

"Out near Moose Creek. With Hal."

Bartoli's brows rose: I lived with a relative I'd loathed in high school.

"Well. My wife's a lawyer, did you know that? You knocked her socks off a couple of times, that Wallace Bean case. Maybe we can have dinner sometime. The four of us?" A tactful inquiry about my relationship with Hal.

"That would be nice." I knew the odds of selling Hal on an evening of small talk were slim. But damn, Jay Bartoli. I wouldn't mind having dinner with him.

"Okay. Well, I'm out of here. But you guys come by the department." A fleeting frown at Sandy. "I heard from Connie Gold you're working for the Clausens. Nice family, the Clausens. Oldest kid goes to tenth grade with my daughter. She's got a big crush on him—always goes for the misunderstood eggheads." He grinned fondly. "Opposite of her jock dad, I guess."

Funny how self-image changes. In 1972, Bartoli would have hated being called a jock.

Sandy seemed anxious to return to McGuin's family. I excused myself, ostensibly to go to the ladies' room. Really just to be alone. I'd gotten used to solitude these last six months. I'd had too damn many people in my face today.

I trudged the corridors, feeling chilled in my damp shoes. From behind half-open doors came the beep of monitors, the gurgle of suction devices, the hack of aging lungs.

More depressed and enervated than when I began, I wended my way back. In the corridor leading to the emergency room, standing with both hands cupped to a sliding glass door, was McGuin's mother. Her shoulders were hunched and her forehead was pressed to the glass.

From where I stood, I could make out parking lot lights but little else; there was too much reflected glare from interior lighting.

Something about Sarah Gowan's posture, tensed to absolute stillness, made me want to find out what riveted her interest.

I stepped through the emergency room's back entrance and walked past a small central island, momentarily bare of nurses and doctors. I could hear voices behind curtained partitions, discussing ailments, explaining procedures, re-assuring children.

I moved swiftly to double glass doors labeled "Ambulance Entrance Only."

The ambulance entry was well-lighted. I peered beyond the dazzle, scanning the parking lot: row after row of empty cars; a Mexican family dashing toward the door carrying a baby; a business-suited black woman and a white male nurse standing under a light, smoking; a big American car driving slowly away; almost out of the parking lot, someone on a bicycle; farther still, the bobbing of a pedestrian's flashlight.

A voice behind me said, "Can I help you?" in a tone that said, Where did you come from?

"I was wondering about Ted McGuin." I turned to find a man in teal scrubs scowling at me.

"Well, we'd appreciate it if you didn't just walk in. We need to keep this area—"

At that point the family with the baby burst through a side door, the receptionist following with remonstrations that they wait until she got some information.

"Mi niña," the crying mother begged.

And the scowling man turned suddenly kind, soothing the woman in heavily accented Spanish, telling the receptionist it was okay, they'd take care of the baby while she talked to the father.

In the bustle that ensued, I backed through the door leading out to the corridor.

McGuin's mother was no longer there.

13

It was almost midnight by the time we picked up the car at McGuin's. Sandy made noises about finding himself a motel room, but I drove us to the cabin. Maybe Hal wouldn't like him staying with us. I didn't care; I'd missed Sandy a lot.

The cabin was dark and quiet, the fire reduced to glowing coals. I poured myself a Stoli, Sandy a Southern Comfort. We sat for maybe half an hour, covered in lap rugs, watching the embers fade. We didn't talk much; just drank, unwound.

I pointed out the guest room, then left Sandy by the cold hearth.

I'd expected to find Hal asleep. But he was propped up in bed, arms crossed behind his head, staring at nothing in the dark.

"You want out, Laura?"

"No. Don't do this." I shed my clothes, too weary to wash the sea salt from my legs.

"I don't need a nursemaid—you know that. I don't need the good life either."

I slid into bed. I tried to cozy up to Hal but found him stiffly unamenable. "I don't care what you need. I'm in this for me, not you."

73

It might have begun that way. But the flare-up of his war injury eight months ago had roused my protectiveness. I found myself monitoring his progress, fearing for him. It was becoming a charade, his insistence that he didn't need me and my assurance that my motives were selfish. The truth was he needed my support, financial and physical. Maybe even emotional, in ways neither of us understood. I didn't mind that. He minded a lot.

"You get this way every time you see your mother," I pointed out. "You offer to end our relationship."

"Yeah, well."

I ran my hand over his chest. I could feel him flinch, my fingers were so cold. "Quit looking at yourself through her eyes."

He moved a little farther away. Had it come out sounding patronizing? Damn, I was too tired to dance on eggshells.

"Sandy and I went to McGuin's house." I explained about the boat, the hospital. Seeing Jay Bartoli. "Jay's going to show us Karen's file—suicide incident report, results of the investigation, coroner's report, that kind of thing."

"Got to hand it to Arkelett—he sucked you in fast."

Fuck. "I watched McGuin's boat capsize. We pulled him out of the ocean. Of course I'm sucked in."

Hal rolled over.

I've thought, at times, it would be better to fight our battles with blatant ferocity, win or lose. I've believed, more often, that retreat is a courtesy I afford Hal in recognition of the fragility of his position. But maybe that's condescending; and maybe that's part of the problem.

I lay in the dark a long time listening to Hal breathe, knowing he was awake too.

14

S<small>ANDY AND</small> I went to the county courthouse first thing in the morning. Though some documents in the sheriff's file were public property, like the coroner's report, others were not. We wanted to accept Jay Bartoli's offer before he thought better of it.

The courthouse was a four-story box—the tallest building in the county. Its cavernous cement lobby was lined with oil paintings of redwoods, the greeting card art of "God's country." We rode the elevator upstairs, and checked in with a woman behind a thick acrylic divider.

A few minutes later, Jay Bartoli ushered us through a cramped file room and into one of a warren of tiny offices beyond. The area had the distinctive smell of police business, of xeroxed paper and lubricated hardware and suspects' sweat.

Bartoli's office was tidy with files and penal codes, the walls adorned with studio portraits of a teenage girl who looked like him. Sandy flipped through Karen McGuin's file as if merely curious, while I distracted Jay with nostalgia. I'd have given anything to reverse the roles. I wanted to see the files, certainly; but mainly, I hated reminiscing. To me the "good old days" meant lying to an old-fashioned father, hoping Diana's acquaintances would not encounter me and report my clandestine outings. Overcompensating for my lack of maternal supervision, the family had tried to cloister me. And so I'd grown up volatile, furious, ready to explode out of senseless social conventions.

I'd exploded out of that frying pan into a disastrous teenage marriage.

Now, I tried to keep my tone light and my smile in place as Jay brought me up to date on former classmates. I tried not to spit when he mentioned my ex-husband.

The whole time, Sandy's words tormented me: I'd put a lot of energy into outgrowing this place. Why had I come back? Hal's sentimental love of the landscape, with which he'd managed to infect me, didn't change the fact that we were back in the family fishbowl.

Or maybe it was a measure of my immaturity that hometown gossip could still trigger the old restlessness. Maybe two decades of wandering had taken care of that for Hal. For all his problems, maybe he was more evolved than I was. Neither of us had made our peace with the past, but at least he'd made his peace with this location.

I talked to Jay, and grew increasingly more melancholy. Hal and I shared so much; we came from the same stock. And all it did was inter us in the same defenses. I remembered his unaccommodating body beside mine in the bed last night. We were defending ourselves right out of mutual attachment.

I was relieved when Sandy closed the file and joined the conversation.

"Interesting case," he ventured.

Jay nodded. "Hard to figure, though. Taking pills, sticking your head in a gas oven, something like that I could maybe understand. You decide you can't handle life and you check out as painlessly as possible. But hell's bells, an ice pick in the face?"

"You think maybe McGuin was doing his wife a favor this time? Giving her a better option?"

Jay wheeled his chair back a foot, still sitting jock-straight. "All I can say is if my wife ever tried something like that,

I'd move heaven and earth to show her how much she meant to me. I wouldn't be putting a gun— Matter of fact, when I first saw the setup, I couldn't believe it happened that way. Didn't believe it, in fact. The dead woman's sitting there holding the gun, but the blast was obviously from several inches away—no powder burns at all. My first thought, to tell the truth, was murder: somebody killed her and put the gun in her hand.''

I sat very still, watching Sandy lounge in his hard plastic chair.

"What convinced you otherwise?''

"Just about everything, which tells you how much you can trust gut feelings in this job.'' He broke into a self-deprecating grin. "McGuin's reaction, for one thing. He was freaking, absolutely freaking out.''

"I've seen guilty men do that,'' I pointed out.

"And I have too. But this didn't feel like that to me. Mostly, you know, it was her history: the fact that she'd tried before, that she'd threatened to finish the job. And the clincher.'' He stroked his reddish mustache thoughtfully. "That suicide tape. I mean, she came right out and said she was going to shoot herself, so . . .''

"So what do you make of this business with McGuin's boat?'' Sandy sounded perplexed, blunting the question's prying edge.

"I went out to the hospital this morning, talked to him again.'' A shrug. "Still says he's not sure what happened. So I'm not too clear.''

"Not clear it was deliberate versus some kind of accident?''

Another shrug.

"Or not clear whether someone other than McGuin did it?''

Jay paused, as if hearing some internal voice. "I try not to make judgments without facts.''

In eight years of practicing law, I'd never met a cop who succeeded in doing that. But Jay's sudden caginess didn't surprise me. Unlike the McGuin suicide, which he seemed to consider settled and closed, we were now discussing a matter still under investigation.

"So how about that dinner sometime soon?" Jay smiled.

"That would be nice." If today's stroll down memory lane was an indicator, I wasn't ready for further reminiscence. (God, was I becoming as antisocial as Hal?)

He opened his mouth as if to speak, glancing instead at Sandy.

Sandy took the cue. "If you'll point me to the gents'?"

"End of the hall and to the left." He waited until Sandy was a few paces past the door. "I mean it about dinner, Laura. And you don't"—a slight flush—"you know, have to worry. My wife knows about our thing, you know, back when. No big deal."

I was surprised he'd even confessed that utterly meaningless and unrepeated coupling. The only emotion I associated with it was a steamroller urgency to cheat on a husband who was cheating on me.

"No big deal," I agreed. And then, to change the subject: "Is that your daughter?"

"Yeah." He beamed at the photographs on the wall. "From my first marriage, but we've had custody pretty much all along."

The photo showed a cranky-faced brunette maybe sixteen years old. It never failed to shock me that people my age could have adolescent children.

"She looks intelligent." Obviously too intelligent to smile vacuously for a camera.

"Oh yeah." He sounded as if that were a mixed blessing. "She's got a mouth on her. Won't read anything but Dostoevsky." He shook his head indulgently. "That's why she's stuck on the Clausen kid. Thinks it's romantic the way he moons around looking tragic. That's her word—tragic. Nerdy's more like it."

I wished Sandy would hurry back. I wasn't good at family small talk. "Well, with any luck, I'll get to meet her sometime."

At which Jay Bartoli pulled out a pocket organizer and suggested I choose a night to come to dinner. I told him I'd better check Hal's calendar before making a commitment.

I felt a sudden desolation. There was nothing on Hal's calendar but me.

15

"**N**O, NOT THE elevator. This way."

Sandy took my elbow, guiding me across the courthouse hall. A glass-topped door was stenciled with the words "District Attorney." "I just checked. Connie Gold, your unaggressive D.A., can give us ten minutes. Right now."

I let him guide me through the door and into an anteroom that smelled of cologne and old carpet. A young woman with a bad complexion watched us through an acrylic wall inset with round grilles.

Sandy told her, "Ms. Gold's expecting us."

A tall, narrow brunette appeared at the glass. "Come on through."

A door to our right buzzed until Sandy pulled it open.

Connie Gold waited for us on the other side. Her long face, horsey with protruding teeth and a ponylike fringe of bangs, seemed frozen. Wariness, perhaps. My reputation doesn't endear me to D.A.s.

We exchanged handshakes, and she walked us past several small offices to an even smaller one. Diplomas adorned one wall; another displayed the usual unimaginative redwood art.

"Let's get straight to it." Her voice meandered in pitch and intensity. I wondered how so distinctive a voice played in the courtroom. "I'm afraid I can't give you much time."

"It's good of you to squeeze us in. Mostly, I just wanted Ms. Di Palma to have a chance to get technical with you. Talk over the legal points."

Thank you, Sandy. "I was curious why you didn't indict Ted McGuin for either murder or assisted suicide." I hoped it didn't sound like an accusation.

"Let's just say we couldn't poke a hole in his story." A momentary scowl. "Or that we didn't have the hard evidence to disprove it."

"What is his story?"

"He denies giving his wife the gun."

"He says his wife was lying on her suicide tape? Her final message to the world?" How unaggressive could this D.A. be? A jury would believe a suicide's last words over the self-serving denial of her husband. Any day.

"We didn't find his fingerprints on the gun," she continued, a trifle crossly.

"Was it his gun?"

"Yes. A bequest from his grandfather, apparently."

"So his prints should have been on it."

"He says he kept it wrapped up and put away. So arguably the prints were polished off in the wrapping."

"Was the gun kept loaded?"

"No. But bullets were in a box wrapped with it."

"Were her prints in all the right places? For loading it?"

She shook her head as if scouring the air with her bangs. "Maybe, maybe not. They're too smudged to identify."

"But you've got her prints on the trigger and stock."

"Yes."

"As if she'd picked it up off the table, already loaded." I tried to keep the statement from sounding like cross-examination.

"Or loaded it herself but her fingerprints smeared."

I tried to see the D.A.'s point of view. "You'd be arguing her word against his."

"With her being demonstrably unstable."

"And him having every incentive to lie."

She shrugged. "I don't have enough to go in with."

The suicide tape and the absence of prints identifiable as hers on the chamber: I'd have gone for it. Who knows what else I'd have turned up along the way.

"Did Karen McGuin lie about anything like this before? Did she have a history of accusing McGuin?"

"No." The D.A. glanced at her watch. "Quite the contrary, I'm told. She made a point of exculpating him in the first suicide attempt, blaming herself for everything. But then, her mental history suggests a pattern of taking on blame. Punishing herself for very minor episodes that she considered mortifying."

"So the fact that she blamed McGuin this time—"

"Obviously, if I didn't give weight to her tape recording, I wouldn't have put my energy into an investigation."

"May I ask, what kind of evidence would you consider sufficient? You've got her statement; you've got the fact that she didn't blame McGuin as part of her pathology. And you don't have her fingerprints where they should be if McGuin's story is true."

"You might be able to defend someone with such flimsy stuff"—she stood—"but you could never prosecute. A crazy woman's word versus the presumption of innocence. A dead woman too; no chance to put her on the witness stand."

As if lawyers who practice in front of juries believe in the presumption of innocence.

Out of the corner of my eye, I saw Sandy fidget in his chair. He needed to continue working with Connie Gold. Maybe I was sounding a little hostile.

"I'm sorry, Ms. Di Palma, Mr. Arkelett. If you have further questions, you'll have to come back another time."

Her tone said, I'll be sure not to be here then. I hoped I hadn't burned out the relationship for Sandy.

Out in the hallway, Sandy observed, "Elevator won't come any faster just 'cause you hit the button over and over."

"Fucking unaggressive cream puff of a woman—how'd she ever get that job?"

The elevator doors chose that moment to yawn open. Sandy stepped in before me, hitting the button marked "Basement."

"Quick five minutes with the medical examiner, okay?"

"What gives, Sandy? What was in Bartoli's file?"

"About what you'd expect. Except for one thing."

"Which is?"

The elevator went down two floors, depositing us in another corridor of banal redwood paintings. Again Sandy took my elbow.

"Which is maybe my mistake. But you tell me if I'm wrong: Didn't your nurse friend say Karen McGuin came in twice to get stitched up? Before her suicide attempt?"

"Yes."

"She didn't say four times, right? She said two times."

"Two times."

He guided me through the medical examiner's door.

"Howdy," he said to a heavy woman behind a long counter. "Is anybody handy to talk to us about file number—" He fumbled in his pocket, extracting a piece of sheriff's department notepaper. He slid the paper across the counter.

I squeezed his arm in admiration. Anyone could order a coroner's report, but there was nothing like official letterhead to get you in to see someone.

The woman spoke in a slow Oklahoma accent, common here since dust bowl days. "If you'll just have a wait."

She returned almost immediately with a chubby man in owlish glasses.

He introduced himself, but didn't offer to take us to his office. He leaned on the countertop facing us. "You have some particular reason for your interest in this case? Not affiliated with the sheriff, are you?"

"We don't need—"

"We've been speaking with the Sheriff's Investigator Bartoli," Sandy interrupted me. The medical examiner knew we didn't need a reason, that the records were public. But saying so wouldn't get us what we wanted. "I just happened to notice something that didn't jibe with the hospital charts." He stuck out his hand. "Sander Arkelett."

The M.E. reluctantly extended his own plump paw.

"You've probably been getting some morbid curiosity on this one, huh?" Sandy continued pleasantly. "I'm up here from San Francisco in the employ of the dead woman's family. Laypeople, you know, wanting to make sure they understand what exactly happened."

"And you are . . . a lawyer? A medical person?"

"I'm associated with the law firm of White, Sayres and Speck." He fished in his sport coat pocket, extracting a business card.

Through Coke bottle lenses, the man examined it. "If you'd like to order copies of the documents sent to this firm . . ." He motioned for the woman to return to the counter.

"Actually," Sandy said, "just a quick question about something: The report says Karen McGuin had four scars on her abdomen?"

The M.E. said nothing.

"Two on the belly, two up higher on the torso."

The Oklahoma woman waddled to the counter. "Doc?"

"Help these folks order a coroner's report," he told her. "It's thirty-five dollars, payable in advance."

Sandy fished out his wallet. "Could I pick it up later today?"

The woman nodded. "Afternoon's good." She squinted at the file number.

"But wait. Sir?" Sandy forestalled the plump man. "I just read through the report upstairs. And I've got a quick question about those scars: The report's accurate in saying there were four of them? On the abdomen, I mean. Not the extremities."

The medical examiner stood in arrested motion, apparently deciding whether to answer or tell us to read the report and leave him alone.

"That is correct, isn't it?" Sandy pressed. "Four scars on the abdomen. That's not a mistake or a misprint?"

"The report does not contain misprints."

"The report didn't mention the scars looking new—you know, fresh or red or anything like that?"

"No, it didn't," he confirmed. And with that, he turned away.

16

MADELEINE ABRUZZI WORE a nurse's uniform today; she looked tired and harried, short-staffed into "working the E.R." She shook her head. "No, I only saw two scars. One high on the belly and the other one, the new cut, just above the navel."

"Would you necessarily have seen anything farther up or down?"

"Oh yes." She looked amused. "Very little body privacy in a hospital."

"But you didn't see her when she was here after her suicide attempt? Or for any of her reconstructive surgery?"

"No. I knew she was here, of course. But in terms of actually examining her, no. Like I told you, I saw her when she came in before that."

"During the suicide attempt, she cut her legs and arms and face, right? No place else?"

"Arms"—she traced two lines on her left arm and a long one on her right—"legs"—she made a few quick strokes on each thigh—"and face." She brought the side of her hand diagonally across her nose. "According to her chart."

Sandy rubbed his wrist with his thumb, looking at the

skin. "How long does it take before a scar stops looking fresh? Stops looking red and new-looking? Just a ballpark guess?"

"Two to four months. For the *redness*"—she emphasized the word, letting us know she remained nontechnical for our benefit—"to fade."

Two nurses approached at a walking sprint. One said, "Multiple vehicle accident."

Madeleine shot me a glinting under-the-lashes glance: I'm important; I save lives. "We'll have to talk later."

I watched her trot away. From down the hall came a thin wail of geriatric misery.

"She used to be skinny and spry," I commented. "Like she was going to effervesce right out of this boring town."

Sandy was blinking rapidly, his pale brows pinched and his sand-colored hair spilling over his forehead. "God damn, I wish we could get access to Karen's mental health records."

"The family couldn't get copies?"

"McGuin is next of kin. He's the only layperson they might give them to. And far as I know, he hasn't made a request."

"No copy in Bartoli's file?" I watched Sandy shake his head in frustration. "They're not exactly busting ass to build a case against McGuin, are they?"

"Nope."

"What are you thinking, Sandy? About the scars?"

"Between the last time Karen came here to get stitched and several months before she died—probably before her suicide attempt—she got cut two more times. And if these folks didn't sew her up, who did?"

"McGuin."

"McGuin," he agreed. "Your friend"—he nodded up the corridor—"said McGuin had a problem about doing more than he was supposed to—too much initiative, I think she put it."

"And you're wondering if McGuin did some home medicine on his wife."

"Right. I'm wondering, did he just stitch her—"

"Or did he cut her too?"

He put his arm around my shoulder. "Christ Almighty. I wonder if it *was* a suicide attempt."

I buried my cheek in his shoulder. Tried not to imagine Ted McGuin slicing up his wife, hacking her face with an ice pick. Tried not to imagine the pathology that would keep Karen silent in the face of maiming abuse.

"I don't know," Sandy murmured. "I don't know what to think. I can see why her family's going nuts."

I felt a twinge of guilt—I'd been stingy in my sympathy for them. Easier to like McGuin's hipper, more artistic family.

"Except, Sandy?"

"Yuh?"

"Did you hear what McGuin said about the reef shark?"

"Considering I was puking my guts out at the time, not much of it, no."

"He didn't sound like a sadist. He sounded like someone in real pain over his wife's mental illness."

"Both things could be true. You know that."

17

TED MCGUIN WAS in a hospital bed cranked to maximum upright position. He was layered in scratchy-looking blue blankets. He looked pale, his skin no darker than unbleached wheat. His black brows and moss eyes stood out in dramatic contrast. He looked more exotic, handsomer than ever. I wondered fleetingly what Karen McGuin had looked like.

"How you doin'?" Sandy asked.

McGuin blinked up at us. "Cold. I can't seem to get warm." He reached a hand out from under the blankets, touching my wrist.

I jumped. His fingers were like ice.

"My body temp's still down below ninety-five. It was eighty-six last night." His eyes danced with interest. "Part of me's pissed: I wish I'd been more alert; I've never seen a hypothermia patient, not a bad one. We got a wino once who passed out in what was basically a big mud puddle, but his temp was about ninety-one; he wasn't too bad. It probably actually helped him that his blood alcohol level was—" A slightly embarrassed grin. "Sorry."

"About?" Sandy drawled.

"I really get into this stuff. I'm just babbling—you can tell me to shut up."

"You get a lot of people telling you to shut up about your work?"

"Oh yeah." As if it were a major understatement. "I forget how squeamish people are."

"I've got to admit," I told him, "I couldn't do what you do—just the noises you hear out in the hall. The smells. A friend of mine is a nurse here—I keep wondering how she can stand it."

"Oh no, it's great. You get to see some very real stuff. I got to watch them crack a chest the other day, open-heart massage. Sorry." I must not have looked like I'd enjoy that. "I guess we're adrenaline junkies, all of us in the E.R." He squirmed in the bed, shifting into a more kinetic posture. "And it's amazing, it cuts through everybody's bullshit. People talk to you about, you know, not just their injuries but their lives, their problems. They're not always honest, but they're genuine, you know what I mean? They might be in denial or covering something up—drug use, for instance— but you see who they are. I mean, the docs come in just to treat them—they're here a short time. The emergency staff does most of the wound cleanup and prep, all the postdoc care—the majority of patient contact. We get a chance to really connect with the patients. You learn a lot. About all kinds of people. It's a trip."

I found myself on a flight of fancy, imagining the range of trauma, the instant connection McGuin described. In my year with the U.S. Attorney and my two later criminal trials, I'd dealt with people in serious jeopardy. I'd learned more, and certainly felt more, than I had in all my years with White, Sayres & Speck abetting the contrivances of bankers.

McGuin watched Sandy, his glow suddenly extinguished. "Thanks for last night. Thanks a lot."

"Glad to help. You up to talking about it?"

McGuin seemed to flatten against the bed, his head pushed into the pillow as if by great velocity. "I really don't know what happened."

"You must have seen the flashes, the smoke." Sandy

scooted a molded plastic chair toward me, grabbing another for himself. He placed his less than a foot from the bed.

"I don't know. It's kind of a jumble in my mind." McGuin's face, so expressive a few moments earlier, was now carefully blank.

"So tell me about the boat, at least. Inflatable, I gather?"

"Yeah." He looked pained. "Just a little six-foot dinghy. Karen got it for me two years ago. I was saving up for a bigger one. I'd like to get a motor, build a winch to lower it down the hill, maybe. Or a shed above high-tide line."

"But your six-footer didn't have an engine. Essentially, it was an inflatable rowboat?"

"Inconvenient for diving, not to have an engine." A wry grin. "But I have to keep telling myself, one step at a time. I could carry it and the oars down, and that was good. Good exercise, although you need calm sea if you're going to leave the cove. And it would seat one other person. Take a picnic lunch out there, couple of fishing poles." His face clouded.

"Karen go out with you?"

He shook his head. "Rarely. I tried to get her to move too fast on the diving. It just made her . . . resistant. Reluctant to go out on the water." A moment of silence. "I can be a jerk sometimes—I get too hyped. It would have been so great to have her for a diving buddy. I ended up pushing too hard, fucking it up for both of us."

And who, I wondered, had shared his boating lunches?

I heard a hesitant shuffle behind us. A tentative "Hi."

McGuin's face broke into a dazzling smile, and I turned to see Wyatt Lehommedieu standing in the doorway with a chess board under his arm.

McGuin extended an arm, pretty much forcing me and Sandy to stand so he could embrace his father. "Look at you!" he said. "Where's your beard?"

Lehommedieu grinned, running his knuckles over his chin. "It turned white on me. I looked like an old goat."

McGuin's laugh was hearty, crinkling the skin around his eyes. "Sorry I was so out of it last night. Tell me again about the commune. While I beat you at chess."

"Well, that shouldn't be hard." Lehommedieu raised his

strawberry-blond brows. "You know, not one person at the commune played a good game?"

McGuin laughed again. "That should have told you something right there."

"And you probably played a hundred games with Ricky this year!"

McGuin looked like he'd been slapped. Seemed to shake himself out of it. "So do I get to be black?"

His father glanced at us. "I'm always black. It makes me feel hip." Every time he grinned he looked like a teenager with unlikely sags beneath the jaw. Hard to believe this skinny, freckled man was father to the brick-solid, light-skinned black man in the bed. Except for a gleam in the eye.

"Well, it looks okay." McGuin stroked his chin, staring at his father's clean-shaven face.

"Remember when you shaved yours off?" Lehommedieu sat in the chair I'd vacated. He began setting up chess board and pieces on the chair that had been Sandy's. It was so unself-consciously bad-mannered that Sandy caught my eye and smiled.

Lehommedieu glanced over his shoulder at us. "Ricky took a bunch of Polaroids. Ted had never shaved before; he'd had a beard his whole life since it first grew in."

"The hospital has a no-beard policy," McGuin said sourly. "Not for the docs, just us peons."

"He was miserable!"

"I didn't look black anymore." His tone said, Of course I was miserable. "Karen said I looked Sicilian. Or Portuguese."

Sandy shrugged. "Good-looking people."

"I look older."

Lehommedieu's laugh resembled a cartoon chuckle. "He's thirty. What does he know about older?"

"I don't look . . . I don't know . . . I look like a straight, older guy."

"And you laugh at me for needing to play the black pieces to feel hip. Besides, we're finishing last year's game, so I have to be black."

Sandy changed the subject. "We were just getting the story on last night."

McGuin watched Lehommedieu set up the chess pieces.

"You were saying it was a six-foot inflatable?" Sandy prompted.

McGuin looked up at him—reluctantly, I thought. "Right. I paddled out a half mile, maybe. I was paddling back, and all of a sudden I was in the water."

"In the ambulance you said you saw a flash in front of you. We could see it all the way from shore. And some smoke. You must've seen that. Smelled it."

"All I remember is being in the water and thinking I'd better swim for it."

I visualized the plumes of light, the coils of smoke. I recalled him swimming around the ragged remains of his boat. Surely he couldn't have forgotten that.

McGuin watched us. It struck me that on virtually every other subject, he'd been chatty almost to the point of monopolizing the conversation. On this topic, he seemed determined to be reticent.

Was it consistent with blowing up his own boat? Would too much detail lead us to discover his method?

"When do you get out of here?" Apparently Sandy had given up on getting him to volunteer more information, at least for now.

"This afternoon, with luck. My temp should be back up. And I've got enough background to know if there's a problem. Get my butt back here."

"Well, we'll let you get on with your game then. Catch you later on, maybe."

There was a flicker of something—apprehension, annoyance—in McGuin's eyes.

Lehommedieu had finished setting up the board. It was laid out as if in the middle of a game.

Lehommedieu tracked my stare. "We left a game unfinished last year," he explained. "I'd just taken back this move." He executed an L shape with his knight, then retraced it. "After Ted pointed out I'd be checkmated in four more moves."

"Isn't that the point?" I inquired.

"No!" McGuin looked appalled. "I don't want to beat his ass because he made a dumb move! I want him to lie there royally pissed at himself while I hold the spear over him. I want him to know his best game was not good enough!''

The men glanced at each other, the excitement of competition arcing over them like an electric force. Both broke into broad smiles.

We left them to their combat.

18

I LOOKED OUT over the undulating silver-gray blanket of water. On the horizon, gray met gray with nothing but a sparkling ribbon of reflected light to show where sky ended and water began. On my left, a thick band of shifting white foam showed the tide line. Beyond it, the beach gleamed like dull lead. The steep hill to McGuin's house was shagged with every conceivable shade of green.

"Pretty area," Sandy commented.

"You can't imagine," I agreed. Early morning rambles with Hal had taken me over trails and beaches that were impossibly beautiful, soul-savingly beautiful.

"I guess it's always a trade-off, huh? Can't be much to do here at night."

"No." It could be downright excruciating, wanting a hit of crowd energy. There were days I'd have traded my car for a colorful hour in Chinatown or an evening of Berkeley bustle. "But that's always true, isn't it? Nothing's ever fine the way it is. Everything has a significant downside."

Sandy stared at the sodden wood bottom of our rented fishing boat. Gravel and slivers of wood made a murk of a quarter inch of water.

He held the tiller of the small outboard motor, throttle turned low as we floated in the steel ball luster of unusually calm water.

He looked like he was going to say something I didn't want to hear. I inhaled a lungful of cold air.

Sandy seemed to think better of whatever he'd planned to say. He scanned McGuin's hillside again.

"Who knows what the tide did with the rest of it," he muttered. "Hopefully this bit'll tell us something."

In the front of the boat was a long strip of thick yellow fabric, somewhere between canvas and vinyl in texture. We'd also collected a piece of singed duct tape the same color, maybe three inches wide.

"You ready to head back?"

I nodded. I'd been ready for the last chilled hour, ignoring numb lips and cheeks, ignoring the queasiness of constant bobbing. It had been worth it for the view, though. Worth it to scan miles of water that looked like mercury, miles of beach rising into lush hills.

"I wish I knew how to scuba dive," I heard myself say. "Just to know what it looks like under there, to be able to visualize it—wouldn't that be something?"

"Not for me," Sandy said, twisting the throttle and shooting us toward shore. More loudly over the engine's din: "I'm a land mammal—doesn't seem natural to trick myself up to be something else." He stopped the boat suddenly, tensing to full, straight-spined height. "What's that?"

I followed his gaze. Someone stood on McGuin's hillside, a small black silhouette against the pearl sky.

"McGuin's got a visitor." It was too far to guess whether it was man or woman.

Again Sandy hit the throttle, sending the boat slapping toward shore. The figure disappeared before we made it even halfway in.

Close to shore, Sandy slowed, then cut the engine. He hunched over it a moment, tipping the outboard forward, out of the water. Then he reached for a pair of scarred oars on the boat bottom. He slid them through steel rings and began dragging them through the heavy water.

Within minutes, his face broke into a sweat and his breathing grew labored. Even after four years his lungs hadn't quite recovered from two bullets in the chest, courtesy of Wallace Bean's vigilante.

When the boat touched bottom, frothy tide still swirling around us, Sandy peeled off his shoes and socks, rolling up his trouser legs.

"Give me ten minutes to go up there and check it out." He handed me the oars. "Use these to keep us on shore."

"Okay." I wasn't in the mood to get my legs wet. And the hillside figure had probably left McGuin's by now.

"But, Sandy?"

"Yuh?" He tucked shoes and socks under one arm, looking crankily at the cold tide.

"I'm freezing. Don't be long, okay? Or if you're going to be a while, come back down and tell me?"

"Not more than ten minutes," he promised. "I'll wave and let you know if I'll be longer. Okay?"

"Okay." He knew how much I loathed waiting. But one of us had to remain with the boat. We didn't want our ride back to the rental dock to wash away without us.

He swore as he climbed into the cold surf, hastily splashing through it. Then blotted his feet with his socks and slipped his shoes on.

The boat surged away from shore with the next wave. It took me a few awkward moments to manipulate the oars and push myself back onto the sand.

Sandy was halfway across the beach now. He turned and waved, cupping his hands to his mouth and shouting. I caught, "Hang in there," and, "Ten minutes."

The complications of staying on shore without leaving the boat made the time go quickly. When I glanced at my watch, I was surprised to find that fifteen minutes had passed.

I scanned the hilltop, seeing no sign of Sandy. Had he gestured to me after ten minutes? I cursed my stupidity for not keeping a closer watch.

It was another five minutes before I began to be alarmed.

I watched the hillside with such raptness that every time I blinked, I saw the scene in negative.

The wind was coming up, stinging my cheeks with spindrift and needles of sand.

I watched the hill and worried. Remembered finding Sandy in a gully beside Uncle Henry's house, bleeding into the pleats of his tuxedo shirt. My partner. Shot because of my "success" in the Bean case.

Memories of other aspects of our partnership: weekend trips together, champagne and Jacuzzis; talking politics, office personalities, subtleties of cases, ironies of "justice."

I was getting scared. Wondering if my dread had some extrasensory basis, if on some cellular level I knew my partner was in trouble.

I yanked up my pants legs, kicked off my waffle-bottomed loafers and thick socks. I wrapped them in the yellow vinyl of McGuin's boat, making sure the bit of duct tape was in there too. I hoped we didn't lose the boat. But if we did, there was no sense losing our haul as well.

The shock of water on my feet sent a jolt through my system. My inclination was to get the hell out. But I bit my lip and muttered oaths and pulled the pointed end of the boat with all my strength, trying to anchor it more firmly on the beach.

I sweated through my cotton shirt and into my woolly sweater. My legs were numb to the knee, the rest of me clammy hot. But I finally got the boat to stabler sand.

I carried the remnant of McGuin's dinghy about halfway across the beach before I unwrapped it, letting my loafers drop to the sand. I slipped them on quickly, tucking the strip of vinyl under a trunk of driftwood.

Then I ran, frightened for Sandy beyond any rational basis for fear. I scrambled up the hillside in a panting frenzy, pulling myself on barbed stalks and tangles of brush to increase my speed. My fingers were too cold to feel the scratches.

I was conscious of the pounding of my heart as I raced through McGuin's yard, checked his porch, tried his door and found it locked.

I backtracked quickly to the shed.

The rough-timbered double doors were closed but slightly ajar. I jerked a rusty latch, opening one door. The windows over McGuin's workbench showcased the far end of the shed. Tools caught the light, jars of nails and powders reflected outdoor greenery. Closer to me, the shed was in shadow.

So I almost fell over Sandy on my way inside.

He was lying close to the scuba gear, beside the padded cinder blocks of McGuin's now-capsized boat.

He was on his stomach, hands splayed as if he'd tried to catch himself falling forward.

I dropped to my knees beside him. There was an odd smell in the air, a chemical smell.

But the cause of Sandy's fall was apparent. His hair was caked with dry blood. Not a lot, and the bleeding had stopped, but it must have been a hell of a hit to break the skin.

I heard car wheels crunch the gravel of the driveway.

I left Sandy for a moment. I ran to the door and looked out. It was McGuin's Honda. I could see him in the passenger seat, his short not-quite-Afro round in silhouette.

I knew he might be Sandy's attacker, returning. But I shelved that paranoia, needing his expertise.

I dashed in front of the car, causing the driver, Wyatt Lehommedieu, to hit the brake sharply. I ran to the passenger side, yanking McGuin's door open.

"Hurry," I panted. "You've got to look at Sandy. See if he's okay."

McGuin's twitch of irritation (at my trespass?) vanished. "What's wrong?"

"He was hit." I wrapped my hands around his huge bicep, tugging at him. "Hurry."

He followed me into the shed, stopping momentarily when he saw the supine form. Then he bent over Sandy, ear to his mouth. I watched him feel for a pulse. I crowded close enough to merit an impatient push from McGuin as he sat up, gingerly parting the blood-matted hair.

He called out, "Wyatt!"

Lehommedieu stood in the door, blocking light. "Yes."

"Get my first-aid kit."

"Where is it?"

"Same place. Hurry up."

The room brightened, so I knew Lehommedieu had gone.

"What's that smell?" I asked McGuin.

I saw him glance worriedly around the shed. He hesitated a moment before saying, "I don't smell anything."

Lehommedieu returned with a square red bag. McGuin took it from him.

"You need help rolling him over?"

"In a minute." McGuin was emphatically in charge.

He rooted in the bag, pulling out a tiny flashlight. He held it in his teeth as he knelt beside Sandy, his cheek almost touching the plank floor. He gently opened Sandy's left eyelid, aiming the beam of light at the pupil. Sandy's right eye was pressed to the floor, but McGuin insinuated two fingers under Sandy's cheekbone to raise his head slightly. With the other hand he opened Sandy's right eyelid.

He sat up then, pulling a small bottle from his red bag. He looked serious but unrattled. Professional. He said, "It looks good in terms of pupil dilation."

He parted Sandy's hair again, revealing a matted scrape a few inches long. He carefully poured liquid from the small bottle over it. It foamed as it touched the wound.

"Just hydrogen peroxide," McGuin said. "To clean it."

He delicately touched Sandy's head, feeling the skull. His fingers wandered lower, down the back of Sandy's neck and along his spine.

"Both of you get on this side of him. I'm going to hold his head still—protect the C-spine. When I say so, roll him over." He moved Sandy's right arm down.

I crawled a few paces on my knees, positioning myself at Sandy's left shoulder. Lehommedieu squatted beside me while McGuin held Sandy's head straight.

"Now gently, roll him," McGuin commanded.

As we rolled Sandy onto his back, his eyes twitched open. He saw McGuin and reached up to push him away.

"Sandy!" I bleated. "Are you okay? What happened?"

"We should get an ambulance up here," McGuin said.

"No," Sandy murmured. "Wow. Light show." And then, seeing McGuin's gesture to his father: "No. I don't need an ambulance. I been cold-cocked before."

"You could have a concussion."

Sandy was cold-fish pale, eyelids fluttering on the brink of unconsciousness. "Hurts, that's all. I'm okay."

"Try moving your feet and hands," McGuin recommended.

Sandy moved them.

"Know your name and address?"

Sandy rattled them off, his tone ironic.

"What happened to you, Sandy?" I repeated.

His eyes closed. A turn for the worse? A pause to edit his story?

"Looked around a bit outside. Went over and waved to you—ten minutes were up. Then I came in here. That's all I remember." His voice sounded weary.

"We rented a boat," I explained to McGuin, hoping to take some of the pressure off Sandy. "We were out sightseeing, and Sandy recognized the hill leading to your house. Someone was standing up at the top. Sandy came up to check it out."

"Why?" McGuin's voice was tight. Suspicious.

"After seeing your boat blow up . . ." I left it at that, hoping he'd extrapolate some kind of explanation from it. "He said he'd be back in ten minutes. After about half an hour I got worried. I came up too."

"The boat," Sandy said.

"I pulled it as far as I could onto the sand. I don't know." Sandy tried to sit up.

McGuin stopped him. "We're going to get some blankets on you so you'll be more comfortable. I've put disinfectant on your wound, and we should get some ice on it. Then you're going to lie still for a while, until you're feeling better, okay?"

"The boat might—"

"We'll deal with the boat. You're sure you don't want us to call an ambulance? Have a real doc"—a twinge of wistfulness—"deal with this?"

"No. I've been through this before; I know I'm okay. Half an hour and I'll be myself."

"We'll get you those blankets." Then to me: "I should probably stay close to him for a while. Do you want to stay up here with me?" Do you trust me? "Or do you want to go down and deal with your boat?"

"I'll help you with the boat," Lehommedieu offered.

Sandy made the decision for me. "Deal with the boat. I'm okay here."

"You're sure?"

"Go," he repeated. "I don't want to have to buy it."

And Wyatt Lehommedieu extended a hand to help me up.

19

WE SAT ON a pile of smoothly twisted driftwood, drying our feet with sand. Lehommedieu watched me, grinning shyly, eyes dancing with interest. The combination again reminded me of a freckled teenager with crow's feet and a slack jaw. His thinning strawberry hair was damp with sea mist, tousled by afternoon wind. His too-small sweater was unraveling at the cuff, and his corduroy jeans were worn to a dull sheen. I summoned the energy to smile back. It had been a chore, dragging the boat farther up onto the sand.

"What a strange time," he commented. "For the family."

I wanted him to hurry, wanted to return to Sandy, make sure he was all right. I forced myself to be polite. "You've been gone a year?"

"A little over. I've lived in communes on and off since the sixties, but this was going to be different, I thought. I thought I'd finally let go of enough ego to become part of a community." His brows crimped wistfully. "To be totally honest, as much as I try to appreciate other spirits, they suffer by comparison to Sarah and Hannah and Ted. I end up coming home and getting off the path. Missing my master."

I'd wondered, when that parlance was more popular, why people followed masters. Growing up under my "aunt" Diana's thumb, a master had been the last thing I'd wanted.

Lehommedieu brushed sand from his blue-veined feet and fumbled with his sock. "The guru-devotee relationship is probably the hardest in the world, you know. Because it forces you to turn your back on traditional allegiances. In a sense, it makes you choose your family."

"Well, your family—your real family—seems close." *Hurry,* I urged silently.

"I haven't seen my parents or my brother in twenty-five years. They basically divorced me when I married Sarah. And God, she was so gorgeous and so wise—I couldn't believe all they saw was her skin." His shoulders drooped. "I tried one time to reconcile with them. Ted wanted to meet his grandparents, so I took him up to Oregon to their summer place and walked in on them—a real mistake. They were very cold to me, wouldn't even speak to Ted, pretended he wasn't there. Except one time when he knocked over a lamp—my dad slapped him and called him a pickaninny. But"—he brightened—"that's just the family I was born into. Sarah's is the family I chose."

I'd gone full circle, choosing Hal. I thought of him at age eight, pleasing his parents with swimming trophies and home runs; at age sixteen, rejecting as symbolic of them their gift of a sports car. I'd disliked him when he was my "cousin." Only later, seeing how totally he'd shunned us, did I grow close to him. If you could call us close.

"I've worried about Ted at times. I've been in and out of his life. Sarah has too: three years with the Krishnas, a couple of times she went back to New York, that time she broke down. And Hannah, well, she's been with Sarah sometimes, with me sometimes. She married that doctor for a while. And Ted's been fending for himself pretty much his whole life, living all over the place, staying with us, staying with friends—lots of good folks in the world—doing odd jobs as a kid so he'd have food and laundromat money. You know, and then I think about my own background, so traditional and so many advantages. So easy, I guess."

"Your son seems like a very confident person. A very

enthusiastic person." I pulled socks over my numb flesh, not looking at Lehommedieu. Not saying, Your son seems fine— for a man capable of taunting a depressed wife with a loaded gun.

"When you let a child take responsibility for his own needs"—he shrugged—"you end up with someone who knows he can take care of himself. He's not afraid of failure, you know what I mean? He trusts himself. If you don't get that as a kid, you end up chasing after it later."

I saw Hal in my mind's eye. What had Sandy called him? An emotional black hole? A homeless, bitter drifter most of his adult life, proving to himself over and over that he didn't need the privileged cosseting of his youth.

I put my shoes on, stood quickly. Lehommedieu stared up at me, one sock on and one off. Rather than endure his scrutiny, I walked away. I noticed the trunk of driftwood I'd used to anchor the torn rubber of McGuin's boat.

I retrieved the ragged yellow rectangle. I was carrying it to the beached fishing boat when Lehommedieu appeared beside me. "Is that part of Ted's dinghy?"

"Probably. We fished it out of the water."

Lehommedieu unfolded it, hunching close to examine it.

I watched the waves lap in. The ocean was as tame as I'd ever seen it. Even on the other side of Dungeness Head, the open sea side, it was probably possible to converse without shouting over pounding surf and whistling wind. I watched the gray surface undulate and wondered again what was beneath it.

I glanced back at Lehommedieu. He was sniffing the thick material, his face pinched into a frown.

"Gasoline." He sounded bewildered. "There's gasoline on this."

I bent closer. An acrid smell mingled with the salt air.

"That's funny, isn't it?" Lehommedieu scratched his forehead at the hairline. "It's on the inside."

I noticed that the fabric was slicker on one side than the other. "Maybe it floated through some boat oil or something."

"I've been wondering, you know, what would make the

rubber pop like that. Ted hasn't been up to speculating, but I keep chewing on it."

"You think someone poured gasoline on it?"

"No. It's on the inside, see?" He rubbed his fingers over it. "It smells, but there's no stain or smear."

"It's been floating around out there since—"

"That shouldn't make a difference. Gasoline's not water-soluble." He stared at the fabric, every trace of frown and worry erased from his features. Blank enough to suggest a meditative state.

"There was some duct tape with that. Do you have it?"

For a moment he showed no sign of having heard me. Then he lifted his other hand to reveal the strip of singed vinyl.

He held it up to the white sky, staring at it. "Yes," he said.

"What?"

Lehommedieu slumped, lowering the tape. He shook his head. "Nothing—I don't know."

"We should get back up there."

"Your friend. Of course." He refolded the tape into the rubber, placing them between the fishing boat's plank seats. "You won't want to take this boat back now—it's getting late. We should ask Ted to check the tide charts, make sure it won't wash away tonight."

Getting the boat back—I hadn't even thought about that. But of course, Lehommedieu was right. Even if it weren't close to evening, Sandy was in no shape for another hour of bobbing and ocean wind. We'd have to taxi back to the car and deal with the boat tomorrow.

"Where did you get it?"

"The marina." Once littered with machine parts and passed-out drunks, now spruced with miniature piers and shivering saplings. Gateway to a bay rimmed with mills, some closed, some still piling redwoods like Holocaust corpses.

"Oh, well, hey. That's right near our house. Maybe Ted can give us all a lift. Or let me borrow the car."

I started across the sand, not caring how I got back. I supposed it would be good to spare myself the expense of a taxi, but after six years with White, Sayres & Speck, I was not in the habit of thrift.

I climbed the hill hastily, adding more chlorophyll streaks to my khakis.

I checked McGuin's shed first, finding it abandoned. Lehommedieu was right behind me with a reassuring "They must be inside. Getting chilly out here, isn't it?"

It was all I could do not to push him aside and run to the house. I didn't know what to think of McGuin.

But Sandy was indeed inside, sitting at McGuin's kitchen table while McGuin, dressed like his father in worn wool and corduroy, stood over him, painting his wound with soaked gauze.

Sandy squinted stoically. "Hi," he said through gritted teeth.

I crossed to McGuin's side, bending close to Sandy's wound. It was a ragged scrape matted with hair.

"It's not bad," McGuin said. "Not on the outside. I think he should go in and get it checked, though. It's possible—"

"It's okay," Sandy insisted. "I don't know why I went out like that. It doesn't feel that bad."

"What's going on?" My voice cracked with exasperation. "Your scuba tank, your boat, Sandy's head—what's all this about?" I squared off against McGuin. He might be substantially wider and stronger, but he wasn't much taller than me. "You've got to know something."

He stopped dabbing Sandy's wound. He watched me, eyes gloomy under lowered brows.

"Did you do any of it, McGuin? Is any of this a smoke-screen?"

"Meaning what?" His voice dropped in timbre.

I felt a hand clamp around my wrist. Sandy.

"I'm okay, Laura. You're just feeling stressed." Don't blow my investigation.

I bent closer to him, sliding my arms around his neck and settling my head on his shoulder. He reached up, running his fingers over my hair. The smell of hydrogen peroxide mingled with Sandy's scents: shampoo, after-shave, the mustiness of the anorak he'd substituted for his sport coat.

"Their car's at the marina," Lehommedieu told his son.

"I'll drive us back to town, if you want. Or you could drop me home and give them a lift out there. So they don't have to deal with the boat tonight."

A brief pause. "Sure."

I straightened, feeling chilled and achy. Angry without knowing why. "Will the boat be okay where we left it? Till morning?"

"It's about fifteen feet from shore," Lehommedieu explained.

"You should pick it up early. Before eight."

I glanced at McGuin. He was staring at his father, apparently unaware of my scrutiny. I took a step backward, shocked by the pain on his face.

Then he looked at me and said, "Damn it! Damn her!" He turned his back and left the room.

"Well, that's natural, I guess," Lehommedieu muttered. "Poor kid."

20

LEHOMMEDIEU PULLED UP in front of the house Sarah Gowan shared with Hannah Arthur. He turned in the Honda driver's seat, saying, "My sense of direction's so bad I'd better let Ted take over."

"It's an easy walk." I glanced at Sandy, wondering if the block and a half from Two Street to the marina would seem easy to him.

His head rested partly on the seat back and partly on his shoulder, which was propped by mine. He'd been leaning heavily against me for most of the twenty-minute ride, eyes closed. I found myself caressing his hand and thinking about a trip we'd taken to Big Sur.

McGuin was in front with his father. "It's right around the corner, Wyatt," he said. "Just drive them, would you?"

From what I could see, he too lolled on the seat, probably feeling the residuals of hypothermia.

"Sandy? Do you want to walk? Or wait here for me to get my car?"

"Rather wait," he murmured. "Bit of a headache."

Lehommedieu climbed out from behind the wheel, apparently oblivious to McGuin's request. He squatted in front of my window, grinning at me and waving an exaggerated goodbye. Then he dashed up the walk, taking the sagging porch steps two at a time. He was pushing open the front door when I tapped McGuin's shoulder.

"Don't worry about driving. If you don't mind Sandy sitting in your car a few minutes, I'll walk over and get my car and come back for him."

"That's okay, I'll drive you." For a moment he didn't move; then he roused himself, fumbling with the door handle.

I was conscious of fatigue and crankiness, of rumbling hunger. I longed to be in my own, very clean convertible, smelling its friendly leather. McGuin's car smelled like old kelp and dirty mats.

Before McGuin made it to the driver's side, I climbed out, ready to reiterate that I'd walk.

Lehommedieu caught us both standing on the driver's side, doors closed.

"Teddy! Hurry!" he shouted from the porch. "It's Sarah!"

McGuin froze, his hands clenching into fists. "No!" he exploded. Then he bolted up the walk.

I ran after him, hesitating momentarily at the threshold. Lehommedieu was nowhere to be seen, and McGuin stood in the middle of the living room, elbows bent and arms out, looking from corner to corner, his eyes huge.

"Mom?" he called, voice so high it cracked. "Mom?"

Then he sprang past a wall of fabric art and into a corridor. I followed.

The corridor was dark, crowded with cabinets full of beaded masks and carved objects. McGuin ran to the farthest door. I watched him enter, stop, audibly catch his breath, and then vanish inside.

I followed more slowly, afraid of what I might see.

I stood in the doorway, drinking in details of the room. Plywood tables were covered with fabric scraps and sorted beads. Two walls were studded with small mirrors framed in brass, shell, wood, enamel. They made a glinting mosaic of the room's draped fabrics and textured hangings.

The fourth wall was bare, hand-painted to look like stone between two large windows.

Sarah Gowan sat on the wood floor beneath a window. She was curled into a fetal ball, forehead pressed to her knees. Her hair caught the light like silver crepe. Lehommedieu was trying to coax her arms free from their vise grip around her legs. He stroked her head saying, "Sarah? Sarah?"

McGuin dropped to the floor beside her. He wrapped huge arms around her, pulling her sideways against his chest. "Mom? What's wrong?" His voice, unlike Lehommedieu's, was a little sharp, a little impatient.

He shook her slightly. "What's wrong, Mom?"

She uncoiled, sliding her arms around McGuin and burying her face against his bicep. She spoke, but her words were a muffled singsong.

"Stop it, okay?" McGuin begged. "Mom? Come on. Talk to me."

She looked up at him. I could see the sheen of tears on her creamy brown skin. A smoker's whisper made her words difficult to decipher. They sounded like, "All that energy, all that fury."

"Whose energy?" McGuin held her far enough away to watch her face. He looked scared.

"Hannah." Her face twisted, and she made a keening sound deep in her throat.

I backed up; the sound was so pained, so primal.

"Come on, Mom," McGuin urged. "You can hang in, you can keep it together, okay? Tell me what Hannah did. Talk to me." His pitch climbed with the last sentence.

Lehommedieu sat back on his haunches looking frightened, letting McGuin deal with it. Hadn't he said something on the beach about a time Sarah "broke down"? Had they been through this with her before, on a grander and more sustained scale?

"Mom, please," McGuin repeated, "talk to me."

She was rocking now, muttering something rhythmic. It sounded like clock sounds, tick tick tick.

"What did Hannah do, Mom?" He folded her into his arms as if the rocking scared him. "Mom, it's okay."

His eyes were closed. If indeed he'd been through this once with his mother, it must have been torture going through it again with his wife.

"Mom? Talk to me?"

"She went to Karen's—" The words came out in panting staccato. "Family. Fury. Where does she get the anger? Ted?"

He held her tighter, muscles bunching visibly through his cheap sweater. His eyes remained closed.

Lehommedieu shook his head slowly, mouthing the words, "Oh, shit."

"Why did she go there, Mom?"

Sarah Gowan pulled back, staring at him. "No," she said.

Whatever she meant by that, McGuin seemed to understand. He looked relieved. "Just the boat?"

"No understanding. Just anger." Her breathing was ragged with tears.

"Just as well." McGuin smiled slightly, stroking her face. "I know it's hard. Be strong, okay?" His pleading tone was painful to hear. "Please, Mom? Keep it together?" *This time*, he seemed to imply.

Her face scrunched, eyes pressed closed, forehead lined, chin knotted. She looked like a child trying not to visualize imagined horrors.

"Mom? Are you going to be okay?"

She shuddered. "Yes. Yes." But she didn't sound convinced.

Lehommedieu stroked her back. I watched him smooth all emotion out of his face and begin mouthing something over and over.

He leaned closer to her, speaking softly into her ear.

She sat back against him, her mouth moving with his. Her face smoothed gradually too.

McGuin held them both, then rose lightly to his feet. "I'll go get Hannah. Don't worry, Mom. How much worse could it get?"

Lehommedieu's forehead puckered momentarily. Sarah Gowan continued her silent chant.

McGuin bent to stroke her hair. Then he turned to leave the room.

He stopped midstride, staring at me. Anger flashed in his eyes.

I stood aside for him to pass. "Sorry. I thought you might need help."

He pushed past me without speaking.

I lingered a moment, looking around the room. The tiny mirrors, the painted stone, the silks and brocades—God, it was lovely.

McGuin was slamming his car door when I reached him. As he turned the key in the ignition, I climbed in beside him. Sandy was still in back. If he was going, I was going too.

Besides, I wanted to know what Hannah Arthur was doing at the Clausens'. I wanted to know what Sarah Gowan meant about Hannah's anger and her energy.

McGuin scowled at me, started to speak, and then shook his head, putting the car into gear.

21

IT WAS CLEAR when we pulled up to the Clausen house that something was amiss. A dented old Datsun stuck half out of the driveway, blocking part of the traffic lane and boxing in two large, well-waxed American cars. The front door was wide open—an uncommon sight in our chilly north coast town—and a red checkered dish-cloth lay across the threshold. As we approached the house, we heard raised voices, Karen's mother shriek-ing, "Of all the cheap manners! Coming to my home—*my home*—"

McGuin jerked as if he'd been slapped. Then he launched himself up the front walk. I was two paces behind him. Sandy remained in the car, tentatively moving his head from side to side.

McGuin entered the house without knocking. I followed, watching him go to his aunt, who stood a few feet from the phalanxed family.

Hannah Arthur looked cross and disheveled, half her au-burn hair trailing from its pins. She wore a sweatshirt gor-geously embellished with the word "Hell."

She swatted McGuin's chest. "I don't need the marines,

buster!'' Her blue eyes filled with tears, which she angrily blinked away.

The Clausens seemed aghast to find McGuin suddenly in their midst. Clara Clausen looked almost feral, a ridge of white defining her nose and ringing her tight lips. Her sprayed black hair was disordered in stiff clumps, as if she'd engaged in a frenzy of head shaking. It seemed shockingly incongruous with her polyester slack suit and the potato masher in her hand.

Her husband stood beside her, lips pulled away from his teeth. He hunched forward, seemed ready to pounce. His son, Mark, utterly conventional in polo shirt and leather sneakers, extended an arm across his father's chest.

In the background, the television blared the theme song of a syndicated lawyer drama.

McGuin watched the Clausens warily, addressing Hannah. ''Mom needs you. Let's go.''

She hit him again, a weak, open-handed slap that barely grazed his solid chest. Seeing them side by side, I was struck by how white they looked compared to Sarah. Had it been a problem for the sisters growing up? Had life been easier for Hannah than for Sarah? Had it contributed to Sarah's fragility and Hannah's anger?

''Well, we certainly did not invite this woman into our home!'' Clara Clausen fumed.

''And the accusations! This is slander, my friend! We could sue you!'' Jerry Clausen strained his son's arm.

''Slander, oh!'' Hannah's hair continued cascading from its pins. ''Care about slander! After you crippled your daughter. Well. No, no. You will not hurt Ted. No more. Time out.'' She shook her finger at them. ''Truly sick and evil people!''

Karen's mother launched herself at Hannah.

Her husband and son were too trussed by emotion to react quickly. I was too surprised.

A person I hadn't noticed stepped into the shrinking gap between the women.

It was Ricky Clausen, the tardy son who'd so angered Mark.

He stopped the attack, his head shaking on his gangly

neck, his eyes opened to glazed unnaturalness, a patina of sweat on his face.

He pushed his grandmother back, clinging to her. She swatted him lightly with the potato masher and broke into sobs.

He turned a bitter face to McGuin, croaking, "You're going to give her a heart attack, asshole!"

McGuin's eyes crested with tears, watching him. He said to Hannah, "Was this necessary? Mom's really upset."

"Necessary, oh!" An impatient slap on the chest. "Where are my cigarettes? You're so naive, you're so Wyatt! Grow up, buster! Who do you think popped your boat?"

He took a step behind her, clamping his fingers on her shoulders. "Come on, let's go. This isn't solving—"

"Oh!" She jerked free. "You don't solve cruel, evil people. These, these . . . Philistines had a treasure and didn't even care! They didn't deserve Karen!"

Ricky Clausen released his grandmother and whirled on Hannah. "He killed my aunt!" His teeth were clenched and sweat beaded his upper lip. "So don't you give me this shit—"

"Ricky!" His father reproved the profanity.

"That's right!" Karen's mother cried. "He's right. You cheap, using, unfeeling— To come to my home and say these things about my family! You—when you live like hippies!"

Hannah fumbled a cigarette to her lips. "Oh yes, yes. Criticizing Karen's hair, her friends, her clothes. That's why she—"

"Clothes! Look at you!" Clara Clausen swept her arm in condemnation of Hannah's sweatshirt. "You get out of my house right now."

Her husband's voice boomed. "You got a hell of a nerve, lady, a hell of a nerve upsetting a woman who's lost her child!"

Into the brief ensuing silence, the television lawyer confidently intoned, "Don't worry, we'll get you out of this mess!"

And suddenly Sandy was slouching toward us, a grimace on his ashen face. He stepped between warring families. "Take your aunt to the car, McGuin, huh?"

An ironic, "Yeah, sure," from McGuin.

The Clausens shifted their focus to Sandy. They began ranting simultaneously: "This woman just walked in here!" "Accusing us!" "This is trespassing—tell her to get the hell out before I call the cops!"

Hannah Arthur had meantime sidled closer to the still-sweating, shaking Ricky. She put a hand on his arm. He yanked free with such force that she fell to her knees.

McGuin moved quickly between them. While the family assailed Sandy, I watched McGuin and his wife's nephew.

The boy's face pulled into a silent Munch scream. He flung back his arms as if falling from a great height.

McGuin's jaw dropped, his face froze. He looked blank, unable to handle more emotion.

I heard Hannah murmur, "Oh my God," and I dashed between McGuin and Ricky, afraid the boy might snap and hit him.

Instead, Ricky Clausen crumpled against me, a loose weave of flailing limbs and sobbing gasps. His voice was barely audible: "You killed her, you son of a bitch. Killed the only one who loved me."

Hannah Arthur moaned, suddenly on her feet again. She reached around me, trying to lay hands on him. "Ricky, we all love you."

I tried to shift him onto his own feet; he was hot against me, his sweat pungent.

I looked to McGuin for help, but he'd edged away. He leaned against a flocked-paper wall.

Clara Clausen was shrieking, "You get away from him, you red-haired witch!"

She knotted herself between Hannah and Ricky, knocking me off balance.

Sandy caught me, moved me aside. He wrapped an arm around Clara and pulled her to his shoulder, keeping her clamped there. Ricky turned his back on them and paced away.

His father boomed, "Quit making a spectacle, Rick. Leave this to the—"

"Grown-ups?" His cracking voice verged on hysterical.

"You're going to let her say this shit to Grandma? Is that what a grown-up—"

Mark Clausen took three fast steps across the room and smacked his son a ringing blow on the cheek. There was an outcry from both Hannah and Clara.

Ricky Clausen tore through the front door. I watched him rage down the walk and across the street, where he hesitated a moment, swiveling his head to the right and to the left before careening on.

"Look what you've done!" Clara, eyes glittering, turned from her son to Hannah Arthur. "You're not welcome here! And neither is the son of a tramp who killed my daughter!"

McGuin stood motionless before his mother-in-law's fury.

I wondered what it had been like before the suicide. Had the Clausens' hatred always been so close to the surface?

"Fucking jig!" the father muttered. "Coming over here! You people always put your business in the street."

And Hannah detonated, flying to him like a comet, red hair streaming. "How dare you, you ignorant, fat, television vegetable! How dare you judge anyone by his color when you don't have the brains or taste of a—"

"Hannah!" McGuin's voice was deep with frost. "You know it won't make a difference. Saying it won't make a difference. How many times do you have to prove that to yourself?"

She turned to him, looking suddenly sad, almost helpless. She reached out fluttering arms.

He stepped into them, ignoring Jerry Clausen's hissing diatribe that she was a bad-tempered, bad-mannered witch who didn't even care about a family's loss, and what kind of low-life hippies would intrude at a time like this anyway?

"Go home, Hannah," McGuin urged. "Mom's upset. Okay? Go home."

Hannah was sobbing, her voice girlish now. "Oh, upset! Aren't we all? Oh."

She allowed him to turn her around and walk her out the door.

Mark Clausen seemed inclined to follow, his lips forming epithets.

Sandy forestalled him by consigning Clara Clausen to his

arms. He was talking fast and low to the family, saying something about everyone calming down now, maybe having some
tea, and they should take care of Clara, try to get her to eat
a little.

I left without saying anything to them. I wanted to make
sure McGuin didn't drive away without us.

He stood at the door of the dented Datsun, hands on Hannah's shoulders while she shakily lit her cigarette, tears
streaming down her face. They looked at each other without
speaking. I fancied the look had a lifetime of uphill battle in
it, of being called "jig": of being angry and fighting back
and having it make no difference.

McGuin closed his eyes tight, apparently determined not
to cry. "Mom's flipping," he said. "Try to chill a little,
okay?"

"Oh, buster. We've seen some bad times in this family."

"Yes."

She wiped her tears, singeing her hair with the cigarette.
"We still have each other."

"Yes."

"And Wyatt's back." She leaned against him. "I miss her
so much, Teddy. I don't know how you bear it."

Silence.

"I miss Ricky, too."

McGuin pushed her gently away and opened the car door
for her. "Go back to Mom," he said. "Don't tell her about
Ricky. Don't tell her he was here."

She was behind the steering wheel now, fumbling through
a tapestry bag.

"Keys are in the ignition," he pointed out.

By the time Sandy stepped outside, Hannah was pulling
out of the driveway with much grinding of gears and squeak-
ing of tires.

Without a word, McGuin led us across the street to his
car. He climbed in. We followed suit.

I stared out the dirty passenger window at ranch-style
houses with apple-pie lawns.

Sandy spoke, his tone neutral. "Your aunt thinks the Clausens tried to kill you?"

"My aunt is . . ." A long sigh. "Hannah hasn't come to terms with it, that's all."

"Come to terms?"

"With the big stuff."

"Your wife's death?"

"Death in general. Ignorance." A weary smile. "Racism. The big stuff. It always pisses her off."

"But you've come to terms with it?"

McGuin scowled at the road, shivering even though the heater blasted. "Let's just say I'm stronger."

I remembered Lehommedieu's theory that a child who fends for himself learns faith in his ability to survive. I wondered if Karen viewed her husband's strength as a comfort or a reproof.

We didn't speak again until McGuin dropped us at the marina. We thanked him for his first aid, but he hardly seemed aware of us.

22

THE LAST THING I needed was more family strife. I pulled my Mercedes up the drive with a resounding "Shit! Both cars. They're both here."

Sandy, limp in the passenger seat, murmured, "Both?"

"Uncle Henry and Diana."

He moaned. He'd been with me when their forty-year marriage shattered. Since then, Diana had wielded their discord like a political bludgeon. It was a testimonial to Uncle Henry's charm and connections that he'd managed to remain mayor, if not evict Diana from the official "Mayor's Residence." Now, four years later, the divorce still squirmed through hearings and depositions. Four years of Diana's bitterness: our legal system accommodated it without strain or astonishment. Those were reserved for my uncle Henry, whose jovial plumpness and sleek black hair were early casualties.

I pushed open the front door, trying to steel myself. But Uncle Henry's sunken cheeks and gray hair once again caught me by surprise. Unlike the glass of Johnnie Walker in his hand.

At the opposite end of the room, upright and overdressed

on my sofa, sat Diana. The tilt of her head accentuated high, arched brows and the thin, curved nose she looked down.

"We've been waiting for you," Hal said sourly. He rose from the wicker rocker. He wore sweatpants and a T-shirt, was barefoot in spite of the evening chill. I wondered what he'd been doing all day. Wondered if I should have checked in with him.

"Hi, folks. Long time," Sandy said wanly. He walked to the couch, taking the hand my aunt offered. He dropped it almost immediately, disappointing Diana's expectation of European attentiveness. He crossed to Uncle Henry, who was sitting in my down chair.

"Sandy got hit by . . . something. Hit in the head."

"An accident," he interrupted.

"He may be a little concussed. He should go lie down." I caught his eye: *Before you get dragged into this*.

As Diana clucked and fussed, Uncle Henry rose and shook Sandy's hand, slurring something about it being "a shame, a shame."

"No, I'm fine, really. Just a little bang—bit of a headache. Nice to see you again."

Hal said, "I'll walk you to your room." *Your room:* Spoken without emphasis, but unmistakably hostile. I hoped the offer reflected a surfeit of parental company and nothing more. I watched the men leave, Sandy trying to keep some lift in his step, Hal trying not to limp.

"So pour yourself a Stoli, Laura." My uncle, after thirty years of congenial governance, couldn't help but play host.

"Thanks." I took his advice. Poured a double. "What brings you guys over?" I almost added, *this time*.

"Well . . ." My uncle looked a little sheepish. He flashed me what must have felt like his usual smile. But it looked different over hollow, gray-stubbled cheeks. (I hoped it was the divorce, not the Johnnie Walker. Because God knew my drink tasted good.)

"We would like to settle the matter of the house privately," Diana informed me.

Right—after turning the rest of the divorce into a carnival. Her lawyer must have reiterated that she had no claim to the house, owned by the city for use by its mayor.

"Thought you could help, Laura. Being family—and a lawyer." Uncle Henry's face was a mask of wistful good cheer.

Hillsdale's city attorney kept urging him to exercise his prerogative—duty even—to throw Diana out and reclaim the mansion.

I looked at her, so cool and coiffed. Trying one last ploy to shame Uncle Henry into ignoring his rights and preferences.

I looked at my uncle, twinkling in his practiced, winning way. He counted on me to present her eviction as a legal inevitability.

I sat in the rocker Hal had vacated, feeling manipulated. I sat there drinking my Stoli.

What were we doing here, Hal and I? There was beautiful country up and down both coasts.

"I've already told you how I read the city charter." I continued sipping.

"Thirty years of our personal finances went into that house." Diana tried to put tears into her voice. "Community property—"

"You're not divorcing the city." We'd been through this before. "But you know I've never practiced family law. I'm not the person to consult."

"During your divorce—"

"Property was not an issue." Did she expect me to side with her just because we shared divorcée status?

She paled. "You might hear me out, Laura. And you might remember that if you'd taken my advice, you never would have married that Gary Gleason in the first place!"

I was reminded of the scorpion who asked the horse to swim it across the river, then bit it midway, condemning them both to drown. Like the scorpion, Diana could not resist using her venom. Like the scorpion, she was a slave to her true nature.

"You know what the law is, Uncle Henry. You don't need to hide behind me."

To give him credit, he didn't do a thirties-movie parody of huffiness, like Diana. He flashed the grin that had worked so well for him over the years. The one that looked like hell now.

Hal reentered the room, his expression unreadable. He sat heavily on the couch, as far from his mother as he could.

I sipped, watching my family over the rim of my glass. At least the Clausens carped at one another and consoled one another and restrained and nagged and hit one another. They didn't politely manipulate one another with charming grins and haughty reminders.

I caught Hal staring at me. He looked tired and grim. Ready, as he had been monthly, even weekly, to let go of the relationship? Ready to tell me again that he wasn't what I wanted? That he could get along without me?

I looked at him and felt exhausted. Weak from holding on to him, from preventing his display of martyred strength.

At that moment I hated them all. I hated their familiar insecurities, hated the way they played out on me.

Look at us: Diana with her dignity, Hal with his walls, Uncle Henry and I with our tumblers. We were bolstered and civilized and utterly separate.

I might as well have been eighteen again. All I wanted to do was run.

23

At seven in the morning, I cracked the door to the guest room and peeked at Sandy. He was sprawled across the small bed, blankets tangled around limp limbs and a T-shirted torso. His lips were parted and his breathing was deep and even. A bottle of aspirin was spilled over the nightstand. I knew he'd feel like hell when he sat up. I didn't want to wake him.

I decided I could get the rented boat from McGuin's to the marina by myself. I could experiment with steering the outboard; there was plenty of leeway out there for mistaken jags and circles. And I could stay close to shore, navigating by landmarks.

I didn't consider taking Hal with me. We'd spent another cold night at opposite sides of the bed, afraid to talk about our problems, afraid the other's view would be painfully harsh. I drove to McGuin's in aching depression.

I found McGuin in his yard, attaching an octopus-like tangle of hoses and gauges to his scuba tank. He wore the sleeveless long john of a wet suit and neoprene booties. He straightened when he heard my car.

As soon as I climbed out, he was beside me. "I don't

suppose I could go out on the boat with you? I mean, I'd be glad to pull it into the water for you and help in any way you need.'' He rubbed his black curls. ''But if you could spare like twenty, thirty minutes? So I could anchor it and dive? Out in the kelp beds.''

All I heard was his offer to help pilot the boat. ''Yes.'' Maybe my relief was blatant. He laughed.

''I thought your friend would be with you and it would be a harder sell. It's just''—he shook his head, still smiling— ''visibility's great. It's been so calm the particulates have settled. And I rarely have an opportunity to boat-dive. The kelp bed I want to explore is too far to swim, so . . .'' His eyes gleamed with enthusiasm.

Within twelve hours, he'd apparently shaken off a major family trauma. Maybe emergency room work trained him to detach from pain. Or maybe that ability made emergency room work possible.

''I'll just be five more minutes, okay?'' He bent over the equipment again, checking hoses and gauges, turning knobs, making the mouthpiece hiss. ''Already checked the spare tank.'' He looked up at me with a grin, putting a huge rubber piece into his mouth and taking a few testing breaths.

I wondered what it would feel like to be underwater, sucking air through a mouth-filling oval.

''You've never dived?''

''No.''

''Oh, it's great. A whole different world.'' He frowned at a valve on the scuba tank, adjusting it carefully. ''I've been doing it since I was twelve—lied about my age to get certified. Not that everyone likes it. By the time you put on this''— he pinched his neoprened chest—''and your jacket and hood and buoyancy compensator''—he pointed to a bright orange vest—''and tanks and fins and all that, you can feel tremendously claustrophobic.''

''Claustrophobic?''

''It's a lot of stuff to be encased in. And the feeling's aggravated by being surrounded by water—it literally closes in on you. It's not your element and you have to be hyper-conscious of it, and that gets to some people. They hate it.''

''You don't have a problem with it, I gather.''

He shrugged. "It's like wearing a spacesuit on a different planet. Part of the adventure is having to be totally careful. It's like left brain's in there calculating and reminding and checking air, and right brain's tripping out going, Whoa, look at that, look at that."

I could feel cold morning air on my face, the smell of sea pronounced and intoxicating. It was a luxury to be with someone who spoke much and easily. It was a luxury to be with someone and not wonder what he was thinking. "I'd like to try it sometime."

"Do you—? I mean, I don't want to pressure you if you're just being polite, but if you want to snorkel around a bit while I'm diving, see what's under the surface, Karen's wet suit would fit you, and I've got extra mask, fins, and snorkel. You could at least check it out. If you want to."

He looked excited, eyes bright and smile manic.

Part of me said, Don't. You don't know this person well and you don't know the ocean at all.

Part of me said, Why not? Why let the habit of caution ruin an opportunity to change?

Change. I was surprised to find myself couching it in those terms.

"Like I said, I don't mean to pressure you, but it is amazing out there. Not so much in the kelp beds—rocks are a trip, covered with life—but still, there's stuff to see."

I visualized kelp rising like a forest of flat leaves and tiny helium balloons. I visualized otters tumbling through it, their sides flashing gold. I looked at McGuin, startled: Had he leaked that scene into my consciousness?

"All right." It came out sounding anxious, reluctant.

"You won't have all this stuff." He tapped his scuba tank. "Just the mask and snorkel. If you stay right on the surface, you don't even have to worry about clearing it. Just keep it in your mouth and breathe through it. You'll get the hang of the fins and all that."

I had a sudden urge to touch his bare arm, see if his vitality was palpable. It had been a chilly, quiet half year with Hal.

"Come on." He walked past me, head down, watching where he stepped in his rubber booties.

He took me into the shed, past the spot where we'd found

Sandy. At the back, near a workbench of tidy jars and clean tools, was an unpainted cupboard. From it he extracted a wet suit.

"Have you ever put one of these on?"

"No."

"It's kind of tricky. Just take your time. The farmer John"—he held up a high-neck overall—"goes underneath. Do you mind getting your underwear wet? I guess I could look for . . . her swimsuit—"

"That's okay."

"The jacket goes over the farmer John. You should wait to zip it and do the bottom tabs—it gets pretty hot. I'll get you into booties and hood and gloves and all that when we're out on the boat."

I looked at the black rubber suit. How tricky could it be?

A sweaty, cranky twenty minutes later, I emerged from the shed. I felt like I was in a full-body girdle.

McGuin stood at the head of the path, scuba gear slung over one arm, stained duffel over the other. He turned when he heard me coming. Smiled approvingly.

"I knew it would be a good fit."

A good fit? "I feel like a sausage. I didn't realize it would be so inflexible."

"When you get a film of water in it, it slides over your skin and feels much much better. The important thing is it's snug. If they're big, they get too much water inside and your body can't warm it. That's what keeps you warm, a thin film of water heated by your skin. Not the neoprene per se. You want me to put your clothes in my bag?"

I handed him the bundle. His solicitousness made me feel I was doing him a favor. Actually, I was relieved to have someone along to handle the boat.

"I thought," he continued, "we could trek over to my folks' afterward. Borrow their car to get us back here."

"Thanks."

"You better unzip the jacket till we're ready to dive. You'll boil." Another smile. "I think you'll like it." With that, he started down the hill.

I followed, aware of every movement in my thick new skin. I tried to focus on the trailside tangle of horsetails and cow parsnips, blackberries and wild daisies. I tried to focus on Dungeness Head, soft with greenery as it curved into the rocky shore. This side of the head, the sea was a languid gray green. Mist pulled the horizon close.

By the time we reached bottom, I was hot with sweat despite the unzipped jacket; more than that, I was anxious. McGuin was right: the suit, pressing and constricting every inch of me, made me feel claustrophobic.

As we pulled the boat into the surf and pushed off, I debated taking the suit off and forgoing snorkeling. It was so unplanned, so uncomfortably unlike me.

But McGuin looked delighted, facing me on the back seat, revving the outboard and turning the long tiller so that we careened over the surf, spanking waves. The shrouded sun painted the sea with a metallic glaze. The boat cut a trough of white bubbles, kicking up mint-colored froth. It was beautiful, and McGuin's happiness infected me.

He spoke loudly, competing with the roar of the engine. "Have you steered this before?"

"No." Sandy, knowing my distaste for the machinery, had done all the driving.

"Come on, I'll show you." He patted the spot next to him on the back seat.

I crossed to him cautiously, kicking aside the folded yellow rubber of his popped dinghy. Neither of us commented on it.

"Turn the tiller in the direction you want the back to point. The opposite direction you want the front to go, in other words."

I took the tiller from him, immediately lurching us off course. I heard myself laugh, a thrilled, scared roller-coaster laugh, and I overcompensated, sending us slapping over swells in a crazy circle.

McGuin took the tiller and pointed us back in the right direction. "It's kind of like doing something by looking in a mirror. Here, put your hand over mine till you get a feeling for it."

I put my hand over his. His skin was cold, slick with sea spray from my wild wake. I was conscious of his tendons flexing as he angled the boat.

"You have to skirt along the waves, not fight them, not bounce over them, but ride them. And keep out of kelp so it doesn't get sucked into the propeller and intake valve. See?"

He grinned at me and I grinned back.

Sandy knew me too well to think I'd want to learn to steer a boat. Hal knew me even better, knew me too well to suggest we rent one.

But by God, I was having fun. Maybe I needed more people in my life who didn't know me, who made no assumptions about what I'd enjoy.

We roared through the water, angling and looping, steering cautiously through kelp. The shoreline receded to a sandy ribbon mottled with black rocks. Rising from a border of dune plants, low hills tumbled with water-fed greenery, cusped with redwoods and cypress. McGuin leaned close, explaining what we were doing, what our strategy was. But every time I took over, we bounced wildly awry.

"I don't do things like this," I explained. "I'm unmechanical. Cerebral, I guess. Document analysis. Legal argument."

"But what's more fun?"

"What I'm good at. Winning's fun. Success is fun." It had been until lately anyway.

"Well, that's a good attitude. That's a good way to look at your work. I bet being a lawyer can be very dry at times."

"Very," I agreed.

"Is that why you're not working right now?"

"No." I considered telling him the saga of my showdown with Doron White, my subsequent firing. But that was just pretext. "Something happened to my enthusiasm. I was doing the work just because I was good at it, no other reason. It wasn't giving me anything and I wasn't putting anything extra into it. I was just being a good lawyer." I looked over his shoulder at the churning froth behind the motor. "I'd been doing that the last few years. It suddenly felt like a long time."

"So what do you do with yourself now?"

How could I explain half a year of brooding walks, of sharing the fireside with a man who rarely spoke? "I used to work with Sandy. I guess he can't accept it that I'm not working now. That's why he's been dragging me around with him, trying to get me back into it.''

He nodded. "That's good." A glance at me. "Maybe. Do you feel ready to go back?''

"I don't know." A long silence. I enjoyed the sting of cold breeze. "I didn't expect to get pulled into this case. But I have.''

His expression grew serious, almost moody. He turned the throttle down, quieting the engine.

"I find myself worrying about it," I continued. "Wondering who you are and how it could have happened.''

He let his hand slide from the tiller. The motor went dead. We floated in the rippling sheen of calm sea. Dungeness Head was well behind us now, framing him like a purchased backdrop.

"What you mean is you wonder why I gave Karen a gun.''

Part of me wanted to say, No. Don't tell me anything you don't want me to repeat to Sandy. Don't tell me anything you wouldn't tell Karen's family. I'm responding to your charm and your buoyancy and the fact that you talk to me and sweep me into your small adventure. But I won't stay swept. I won't stay anything but a lawyer, a very cautious and cerebral one. An aggressive one: I'll use what you tell me. My allegiance has always been to case and client. I've set killers free, I've attached prized possessions, I've shortchanged ailing claimants. So don't tell me too much. Don't get too real with me.

"Yes," I said. "I want to know why you gave your wife a gun. I want to know how she cut herself those two times you took her to the hospital. How she cut herself the two times after that.'' Because it doesn't fit with who I think you are. And I want you to be that person.

He slumped in his neoprene casing, bulky forearms on his knees. "You know about the cuts.''

"Yes. Sandy's very thorough.''

"Have you told the Clausens about the second two?''

"No.''

"I don't suppose you know what a cutter is?''

"What do you mean?''

He looked at me, his eyes glinting. "It's someone who cuts herself. Because of her internal pain. As a way of drowning it out, putting it somewhere physical so she can deal with it."

"Opening herself up so people could see the ugliness inside."

He bent his head for a long, silent moment. "You heard her suicide tape."

"Yes."

"Then you know: she hated herself. And her family—fuck, no matter what she did, it was wrong, it wasn't up to their image of her. They might as well have hated her, they put so little value on who she was." He met my eyes. "I think she couldn't handle it that we loved her—me, my folks, Ricky. The more we let her know how kind and funny and smart we thought she was, the more upset she got. She'd bite her cuticles till her fingers were swollen and bloody—it was awful. Or she'd start pulling all her clothes out of the closet, try on ten different outfits, no exaggeration, then lie on the floor crying, saying she looked so ugly she'd never go out again. That was at first. It got a lot worse."

"Tell me about the cuts."

His eyes widened in horrified remembrance. "The first time it happened, I thought it was an accident. I got home and she was moving strangely, wincing." He squinted at the horizon, a smudged gray line against the pale white of morning. "The thing you have to know about me and Karen was that I wouldn't let up, I just wouldn't let up. She'd get withdrawn, clam up and pull away from me, and maybe someone else would have said, Fine, you need space, take some time alone. But I was in her face—that's just how I am." He kept his eyes averted, as if admitting a loathsome disease. "So she was wincing around telling me she needed space, and I was all over her: What do you need space for? Why are you acting funny, God damn it? And when I brushed her stomach, she jumped like I'd slashed her. I had to pull her sweatpants down to see what it was."

"She'd cut herself."

"She didn't admit that. Oh, fuck. And it was so crazy it didn't even occur to me. Even with her depressive stuff, it didn't occur to me she'd cut herself, you know? I mean, Jesus, a major cut."

I nodded, though I'd never met the woman. I nodded because he seemed to need my agreement.

"She said she'd fallen down holding a knife. I thought it was fucked up of her to be so secretive about it—read her the riot act on the way to the hospital, told her there's a big difference between being brave and being stupid."

A pair of otters popped up beside our boat, exhaling in loud coughs. McGuin mimicked the sound, obviously used to hearing it.

"The second time it happened, I was suspicious. After she got stitched, I was seriously in her shit, trying to get her to talk to me. God. I hated it when she wouldn't talk to me. I used to tell her"—he rubbed his eyes with a savage hand— "Just *talk* to me. If I know what's going on, there's at least a chance I can help, you know? But she was always embarrassed—that's what she'd say all the time, No, I'm embarrassed, please give me some privacy, leave me some room to hide, don't make me share this stuff, I'm too embarrassed."

He sounded angry, looked bewildered. He was back with Karen, not with me.

"And I'd say, Damn, you think just because you're not talking about it, it's not happening? It's not affecting us? It doesn't matter if you don't talk about it, I still have to deal with it, it's still right here, big time. It's like fighting a monster in the dark—I get hit but I don't see where it's coming from. And that's not fair." He breathed quickly, pale with frustration. "But she'd get into this thing of being embarrassed to talk, and she'd get absolutely catatonic, sitting there like a statue with tears running down her face."

His body drooped with recalled helplessness.

"Well, the third time she cut herself, I knew. I knew she didn't have another 'accident'—Jesus Christ. I was going to take her to M.H.U., the mental health unit, because that's the only place open that time of night. I didn't want to wait till morning—and I'm no great fan of M.H.U., believe me."

The boat rocked with a series of swells. McGuin put his hand over his stomach.

"Like I said, I'm an in-your-face kind of person. I was like, Get in the car now, we're getting you some help *now*.

And what it came down to was she begged me to back off. She said please give her a chance to deal with things without doctors stepping in and committing her against her will, probably filling her full of drugs and all that. Please give her a chance to figure things out. Just us alone.''

''But her behavior was so self-destructive.''

''Tell me about it. She was hysterical, threatening all kinds of things. She knew if I took her to the hospital, they'd ask questions, probably end up sending her to M.H.U. She was threatening to kill herself if that happened.'' A long exhalation. ''And I was afraid, really scared for the first time in our relationship. For the first time realizing maybe it was out of my control. Does that sound stupid? That I wouldn't admit that?''

I shrugged.

''I just hate thinking I can't fix things, you know? She was so great when she was up—so smart, so much fun. I kept thinking the down stuff was an aberration, like if I gave her enough love and all that, confronted her and all that, she'd come out of it. But she didn't. And I think that was the first day it hit me maybe she wouldn't. Ever.''

I looked at McGuin, considered his optimism; it would be hard for him to admit defeat.

''She was so freaked. All I could think was there must be a way to fix it. I made a bargain with her, essentially. I'd stitch her myself, wouldn't take her in—she acted like it would be the end of the world if she went in again, almost that she'd die from the embarrassment. I'd stitch her if she went to a counselor right away, first thing next morning.''

''Did she?''

He nodded. ''I made her go every day for the next week or so. I'd pick her up after and she'd be rigid—I'm not sure she even talked to him. I'm not sure she did anything but sit there and feel embarrassed—whatever the hell she meant by that. Sit there absolutely autistic, obviously in major pain. Like she did with me. All I know is, a week later, she cut herself again. And I freaked again. I fucking carried her out to the car kicking and fighting to take her to M.H.U. Because I didn't know what else to do.''

His face crumpled. Tears spilled down both cheeks.

"I hadn't driven twenty feet when she threw herself out of the moving car. She could have broken her neck."

I watched him regain control. Smooth his face, wipe the tears.

"I stitched her up again, and I went back and forth about it. Should I call an ambulance? Let them take her to M.H.U.? But then, Jesus, she seemed so fragile. Begging me not to. To let her keep trying. It was hard. I talked to Mom, and we decided we could always call M.H.U. later. That maybe we could show Karen we were there for her. And of course, watch her. Watch her every minute. Mom came out and stayed while I was at work. My mother's a very compassionate person—she's been there, for one thing. She went through a breakdown herself several years ago—was convinced this terrible *thing* was going to happen to her; she got absolutely paralyzed by it for a while. So she sympathized. And she loved Karen. I thought maybe . . . Maybe I'm too intense, maybe I'm too hard on her, always trying to beat down her walls, trying to get in. I thought maybe Mom could coax her more into talking. I was afraid to do anything else. I was afraid I'd been too aggressive already."

"But she ended up trying to kill herself."

He spoke haltingly. "I don't know what made her do it. I don't know what this big embarrassing thing was that caused her so much pain, or where she got the idea she was ugly inside. All I know is I backed off. She scared me, jumping out of the car. I felt like she was this close to really hurting herself, and maybe part of it was my fault for bullying her and being on her all the time. I guess I hoped if I backed off . . . let her do it her way, let her have some space, some quiet time. Some time with my mom."

He restarted the motor. It's slow whine mingled with the lapping of water, the occasional shriek of gulls.

"Obviously that wasn't a smart move." He sounded glum, squinting at the bright sea. "All it did was make her feel monitored, make her feel more embarrassed. Maybe even glamorized death; made it seem like a way to outsmart us, get away from our scrutiny. She got more quiet and depressed, got to where she was apologizing all the time—all the time, apologizing that we had to stay with her. Saying she knew it must be hell.''

I imagined that it was.

''And then she did it.''

He didn't have to elaborate. I knew he meant slicing her arms and legs, attacking her face with an ice pick.

He twisted the throttle, sent us skating along the side of a big swell. We traveled fast, skimming the water and churning shiny spray.

He turned to me. ''What it comes out to: I fucked up. Majorly. I felt so sorry for her I didn't force her to get the help she needed. Sometimes I think I'm the world's biggest egotist—thinking I could help her myself. Or maybe I just couldn't face it that she was so far gone.''

I wanted to say, Maybe nothing would have helped. Maybe you can't reach some people, no matter what.

I thought of Hal and felt sick.

I put my arms around McGuin. Felt him release the tiller and put his arms around me. I clung to him, sweating miserably in my tight layers of rubber. I clung to him, feeling not a centimeter of his sheathed skin. We floated like that a long time.

When we disengaged, I felt shy, staring fixedly at the bobbing water. McGuin concentrated on restarting the engine, on guiding us smoothly through bloated tangles of kelp.

A few minutes later, he said, ''The kelp bed's right up here. It's rock canyon, where several creeks meet and feed into the ocean. It's great diving when it's calm. All kinds of stuff clings to the rocks. And lots of critters feed on it—seals, otters, zillions of fish. You can reach out and touch them—it's very hip.''

He glanced at me.

''Visibility should be about twenty feet—which is excellent for here, almost amazing. You won't be able to see down to the rocks where the most interesting stuff is, but you'll be able to see the kelp forest and some fish, otters, surface life. It's interesting. I mean, if you had to pick a day—I think you'll like it.''

I was conscious of how much I liked him. I hardly remembered the last time I'd liked someone so much.

I made myself speak, my voice tight with apprehension. "Did you give Karen the gun because you couldn't take it anymore? You were too frustrated?" That's how I'd play it to a jury. Tell him to flash each member that warm smile. Hope the jurors were feeling people, not thinking people.

His spine curled. He stared at the boat bottom, at the folded remains of his dinghy.

"I got it wrong, totally wrong." His voice was quiet, more bewildered than bitter. "I backed off when I should have held my ground. I should have said, You're too far gone to listen to; I'm going to listen to myself. You're fucking cutting yourself, and damn right I'm going to stay in your face. If I'd only— Face it, it was my fault. I should have listened to myself. Taken her to M.H.U. The hell with her embarrassment."

His shoulders knotted visibly in their rubber coat. His posture looked painful.

"Well, I wasn't going to let it happen again. I wasn't going to back off again."

We bobbed in silence.

"So I made a bargain with her: None of this floating-through-life shit. None of this, 'I'll be half alive and mostly thinking of myself as dead already.' None of this pulling away from me." He breathed in quick hiccups, but I saw no tears. "I handed her a gun every morning, and I basically said, You choose life, God damn it. You choose to be here. You choose to be with me and keep on trying."

He slid forward so that his forehead touched the fists on his knees. "Oh, God. I'm such a hard-ass sometimes. Such a fucking hard-ass."

I wondered how long his bargain had worked, how many times Karen McGuin had picked up that gun and thought, No, today I choose life.

I wondered if, on the day she'd chosen to die, she'd have found some other instrument. If she hadn't had a gun in hand, would she have taken up a knife, downed some pills, steered her car into a tree?

Or had convenience been a factor? Had the bargain itself put too much pressure on her? Floating could be so much easier than choosing: Hal was certainly proof of that. He'd made it through the postwar years that way. He'd made it through last night that way.

"You told the D.A. Karen was lying on her tape." The lawyer in me. "That you didn't give her the gun."

McGuin straightened. "I didn't know how to explain this. Not to the authorities." His eyes were bright and beseeching: Do *you* understand? "It seemed easier to deny it. Not even get into it."

"I think you were smart to keep quiet." I slid my hand over his. I couldn't say more. Sandy was right—I'd lost the vocabulary.

He shuddered as if to free himself of invisible entanglements. Then he lifted his hand, mine still atop it, and twisted the engine throttle. I closed my eyes, concentrating on the sleek tautness of his skin.

He steered us to the middle of a vast kelp bed, leaves breaking the surface like vinyl feathers. A family of otters sat head and shoulders out of the water, watching us.

McGuin unzipped his duffel bag, pulling out booties, gloves, masks. Glanced at me uncertainly.

"I've never done anything like this before," I said.

And the enthusiasm was back in his eyes, lighting his face. A man who could let go of pain.

He prattled instructions as he helped me pull on booties and fins, hood and mask, showed me how to bite the black rubber mouthpiece of the snorkel and blow through it.

When he was done explaining how the snorkel worked, how to kick, how to clear my mask, he looked me over, nodding with approval. He looked at me, so uncomfortably laden and encased, and smiled as if I were his very own creation.

It had been a long time since I'd seen a smile like that. At that moment, I knew Hal and I were in trouble.

24

I SLID OUT of the boat with a carnival rush of giddy fear. I didn't feel anything for a moment, only the continuing pressure of the suit, the swelter of being encased in unbreathing rubber. A swell carried me a few feet from the boat, pumping adrenaline through my veins. McGuin popped up beside me like some sea mammal, all black except for a bit of face. Kelp clung to him like New Year's streamers.

"Okay so far?" he asked.

I bobbed, sunk low, a sudden gush of water coming between my face and hood, spreading through my suit like an Arctic chill.

"Cold?"

"Yes," I said. "Almost feels good. I've been so hot."

"It shouldn't take but a minute or two to warm up. Unless the suit's a bad fit. I'll stay with you awhile to make sure it's okay."

"Yes." Thank you; I am truly scared. Scared and thrilled and curious, every synapse firing, every inch of my skin talking to me.

I looked around. Funny to see the ocean surface at eye level, dancing with glossy seaweed.

"Try your snorkel."

I reached for the fat tube attached to my mask. I bit the rubber mouthpiece, blowing out, sucking in.

"Put your face in the water."

I felt McGuin gently press the back of my head. My feet felt leaden and awkward in their heavy fins.

I put my face down, taking a tentative breath through the snorkel. The coldness of the water no longer seemed a relief. It wasn't as bad as I'd expected, but I hoped it would warm up soon.

The snorkel worked. I could breathe, keep my face underwater and breathe. I wanted to laugh: Laura Di Palma looking down into a kelp forest. The sunlight caught waving stalks, gleamed on their slick surfaces. Glistening particles rose through water vibrant with amber light and shifting green opacity. It looked like a swaying jungle, the light fading to semidarkness at five feet, darker at ten, the merest shadow of movement at fifteen feet. I straightened my body, flapping the awkward fins so that I turned.

Everywhere I looked, huge stalks of kelp moved with the tide, descending farther down than I could see. Some were thin with long, individual leaves. Some were fat masses of tiny, splayed leaves. Some unfurled like purple-brown scarves. Some rose like bulbous buoys topped with flat tresses. Particulates swirled like glitter. I caught a tumbling flash of gold: otters playing, nipping and coiling around each other. Real otters.

And then the scary realization: My face is in the water. In the cold northern ocean. I bobbed my head up, let the snorkel fall from my lips. Inhaled with my mouth open and swallowed briny seawater.

McGuin was still beside me. "Okay?"

"Yes. Yes." I was panting, treading water. "It's beautiful."

"Good. Warm enough?"

"Yes."

"Be careful swimming through kelp. Either flatten it with your hands and glide over it, or part it before you go through."

He pulled himself back into the boat. He smiled down at

me a moment, buckling a belt strung with lead weights around his waist. Then he hunched over his air tank, strapped to a metal plate on his orange, semi-inflated vest. He checked hoses and gauges again, then turned the vest upside down, threading his arms in and grasping the tank with both hands. He lifted vest and tank over his head, settling them on his back. When the vest was firmly buckled across his chest, he stepped casually over the side of the boat.

With a loud splash, he sank out of sight. A moment later, he bobbed up beside me. "Hi."

"Hi."

"You won't go far from the boat?"

"No." Believe me. "My mask got tight."

"Exhale through your nose. That equalizes the pressure." I tried it. "Better."

"Okay then. I'll probably be twenty, thirty minutes, depending how my air goes."

"How much do you have in there?"

"Depends on how efficiently I breathe. It lasts longer if you stay calm and breathe evenly. Helps that I didn't swim out. Usually I swim maybe fifteen or twenty minutes to get where I want to dive. So I'm breathing heavier and my air doesn't last as long." He reached for a gauge dangling from his vest. "This tells me how much I have left."

I watched him pull his mask up from around his neck. He positioned it carefully, pinching the clear plastic over his nostrils. "So I'll see you in a bit, okay?"

"Okay." I tried to relax, to float in the "soup."

McGuin clamped his teeth over the rubber end of a teacup-sized circle of chrome. He held up a short hose attached to his vest, pushing a button on the end. I heard the hiss of released air as he sank out of view.

I bit the snorkel again, clearing a space in the surface mat of kelp leaves. Submerging my face, I watched McGuin descend in a cascade of air bubbles. The sound of his breathing was magnified by the water; he sounded like a water cooler. I watched his bubbles rise, watched him linger awhile at five feet, awhile longer at ten. By the time he'd gone maybe fifteen feet, kelp stalks and leaves obscured all but a few bubbles, a few flashes of orange from his vest.

I grasped kelp stalks, needing to feel anchored. Then I began sidestroking, feeling the wind freeze my cheeks, the rest of me finally warm. It pleased me that McGuin was right: the neoprene suit moved with me now that the inside was wet.

I put my face back in. I did something wrong and inhaled seawater. Got kelp in my mouth. Tried again and got the hang of it.

I parted massive, intertwining tendrils and glided between them. I stared into the stirring canopy of vegetation, flattening it with my forearms, sliding over it. I snorkeled in widening circles around the boat, watching sunlight play on translucent leaves and rising particles. Now and then the light formed a moving wheel of rays, each oscillating like a tiny searchlight. I floated, transfixed by the otherworldliness of it. Occasionally I spotted otters playing.

I was close to the boat, trapping cypressy kelp between my fingers, examining tiny air bladders that looked like strings of beads. Looking down, I glimpsed the orange of McGuin's vest. I'd lost track of time, but supposed it must be twenty or thirty minutes since he'd gone under. I was surprised to feel no relief, to feel only disappointment at the prospect of returning to the boat.

I expected to watch McGuin swim slowly to the surface, as divers do in Jacques Cousteau specials.

Instead, the orange vest began rising like an empty bottle, blocked momentarily by thick tangles of kelp.

McGuin seemed to do nothing to facilitate his ascent. His limbs were splayed, moving with underwater tides, drifting like the kelp stalks as he rose to the surface.

It didn't look right. Even to a know-nothing novice, it didn't look right.

I swam toward the spot I thought he'd come up. He was almost at the surface now, maybe fifteen feet in front of me, forty feet from the boat. His head was tipped forward, offering no resistance to the water.

I got tangled in kelp, felt a twinge of panic. I tried to inhale through my nose and filled my mask with water. I couldn't remember how to clear it, felt like I was drowning. A swell filled my snorkel. I spit it out, clawed the mask down around my neck, blinked stinging water out of my eyes. Another swell slapped my face. I sputtered, trying to calm down. I'm a land animal, I thought. What am I doing out here?

I spotted McGuin. A trick of the current put him farther from me than I'd expected. He was partially out of the water, his face and some of his chest visible. He floated limply, swells washing over him.

I called to him. No answer.

I pulled myself along the kelp, trying to hurry. I could see now that his eyes were closed. His mask was half full of water. The chrome circle was still over his mouth, but his lips were parted around the rubber mouthpiece.

With a few kicks of my finned feet, I reached him.

"Come on," I heard myself beg. "Ted."

I pulled the chrome and rubber contraption out of his mouth. It began sputtering when it hit the water, bubbling a strange jig at the end of a hose attaching it to the tank. Its miniature, probably a spare, floated beside it. Seawater washed over us, filling McGuin's mouth and mine. I grabbed his head, lifted it farther out of the water, pulled off his mask and let it sink into the kelp.

Within seconds, he was spitting water and gasping for breath. His eyelids fluttered open, closed again.

I raised his head above the next swell, cold wind rippling the ocean surface now, stinging my cheeks.

His eyes opened. He blinked water out of them. He coughed, then inhaled and coughed again.

I held his head high, rode the next few waves with him. I watched him take deep breaths, look at me round-eyed and confused.

I grabbed his vest, swimming us both toward the boat. I pulled his weight for maybe ten feet before I felt him put some energy into it, before I felt him swim with me.

By the time we reached the boat, he was still coughing a little, but he was definitely with me. I didn't have to help him on board. He crawled in before me, in fact, offering his arm for me to climb.

He lay on the bottom of the boat, head against a benchlike seat. I tried not to flop onto him, but I wasn't used to fins, wasn't used to a rocking boat, couldn't get my balance. I kicked the fins away, tore my hood off, unzipped my neo-prene jacket.

Claustrophobia. I had it in spades.

"Are you okay? What happened?" I panted.

McGuin sat up, holding his head. He leaned over the side of the boat, retching. The sound of it made me ill too.

When I got my stomach under control, I sat back on my knees. McGuin had removed his hood, his thick curls matted and glistening. The wind had come up, whistling in my frozen ears.

"What happened to you?" I repeated.

He slid up onto a bench, shivering slightly, looking at me with shocked eyes. "I don't know. I was down there, and next thing I know, I was up on the surface with you."

"I watched you come up. You looked unconscious."

He winced, touching his waist. "My weight belt—oh, shit, I remember. I remember this split-second feeling of drifting off. I must have dropped my weight belt."

"To get yourself back up."

"I don't remember thinking about it. It must have been an automatic response, unclicking the belt. I wasn't even think-ing, I just reached down and did it."

"Has this ever happened to you before? Did you run out of air down there?"

"No." He reached over his shoulder and grabbed a handful of hoses. He checked the gauge dangling from one of them. "No, it says I have air. I check it constantly. I just . . ." He shook his head.

He sat there a minute scowling. Then he closed his eyes, looking weary.

He unbuckled his orange vest and slipped off his tank, turning so that he was beside me on the boat bottom. He untwisted the octopus of hoses from the top of his tank. They lay across his lap like some robotic sea creature.

Without looking, he groped behind him, feeling for some-thing in his duffel bag. A moment later, he produced a tiny screwdriver.

He bent close to the piece I'd removed from his mouth. He fit the screwdriver into a small indentation at the top of the chrome circle, giving it a few quick turns. Then he fit it into an indentation at the bottom. He said, ''Too easy,'' when the mouthpiece came apart.

He shook the disassembled piece savagely. A slimy object dropped out.

My first thought was that some small invertebrate had found its way into his equipment.

But McGuin held the object on the palm of his hand. It was a thick piece of gauze partially encased in sticky gelatin. Gelatin resembling the capsule coating of bath oil beads.

He held the gauze close to his nose and sniffed. His face fell. He slumped against the bench.

''What is it?'' I was scared. The look on his face scared me.

''Soaked in something,'' he said. ''Ether probably. Positioned partway into the air inlet valve. The other part would get wet enough for the gelatin to melt away. Then I'd be breathing through the gauze. Pulling in chemical every time I inhaled.''

His fist closed and he raised his arm, flinging the gauze out to sea.

''Wha—!'' I reached out, as if I could pull the gauze back by touching its trajectory. ''Why'd you do—?'' I scanned the ocean surface, looking for it. ''Why?''

He let his head rest on the bench and pressed wet fists to his temples.

It didn't make sense. Did he throw away the gauze because it wasn't ether-soaked? Because he'd staged this? Was I just an audience, corroboration for more lies he meant to tell the D.A.?

''Did something really happen to you down there?''

McGuin's eyes blinked open. ''I don't want anyone to know about this.'' He gripped my arm. ''Don't tell anyone.''

''Let go.''

''Don't tell anyone about this.''

''You're hurting me.''

He released my arm, letting his head rest against the bench again. He stared up at the sky.

He was so exotic-looking. Beautiful, really, with his Polynesian-brown skin, his dark brows and wide eyes. But I couldn't read him. Couldn't figure out what, if anything, had just happened.

I felt mummified in my wet suit, my body hot, my face and ears chilled.

I fumbled through McGuin's duffel bag and found a towel, found my clothes. Got myself out of the neoprene jacket, drying my arms as the wind hit them. I turned my back on McGuin, tugging at the Velcro of the long john, hastily drying my torso and pulling on my sweater. I wriggled free of the rest of the suit with unspeakable relief, the towel around my waist. I pulled on my pants. It seemed the height of luxury to wear nonconstricting fabric again. The height of luxury to be surrounded by air, to breathe in and out without thinking.

I kicked the wet suit to the front of the boat, taking time now to blot my hair.

I sat on the bench beside McGuin's head. I watched him as I pulled on my socks and shoes. He continued staring at the sky, water dripping from his curls, beading on his forehead.

I felt chilled and exhausted, bottomed out after an adrenaline rush. I didn't understand what had happened and I didn't know what to think about it. I tried to let go of our earlier rapport so I could be objective. I tried to decide if I'd been used.

I watched McGuin and fought a strong desire to hold him, to console him.

I wanted to trust him. I told myself I knew better.

25

We were less than twenty minutes from the marina. I steered the boat while McGuin unself-consciously peeled off his wet suit.

He pulled on a fisherman's sweater and gray sweatpants. Then he sat beside me and took over navigation, guiding us expertly to the dock.

While he connected the boat to winch hooks, I took my sea legs across a wharf just big enough for a rambling shack combining a bait and tackle shop, minimarket, and fish-smoking hut. Opposite was a row of rental skiffs and a powerboat for charter. The dock smelled of fresh catch and, more faintly, of distant pulp mill. Past the marina, in the bay, lumbermills filled the horizon with white billows of smoke. Digesters, mazes of pipes, low buildings with whitewashed windows, glinted as far as the eye could see. Lumber was stacked for shipping or heaped into mountains of chips.

I did the best I could with rest room soap and mirror, then settled the bill with the boat shop. I found McGuin standing with duffel bag bulging at his feet and tank vest open over his sweater.

He looked tired, almost ill. "Would you mind taking one end?"

I grabbed one handle of the duffel and he grabbed the other. We made slow progress along the short pier and new bricks of the "marina park." We walked past intricately repainted hotels that had once been flophouses.

A few minutes later, we reached his family's sagging Victorian. McGuin carefully deposited the duffel bag and scuba tank beside his aunt's Datsun.

Then he faced me, taking both my hands. I suppressed a fleeting desire to touch his arms, his chest.

"It's up to you," he said. "You're the one who got me out of the water. You have a right to be part of this, if you want."

"Part of what?"

"The family has to talk."

Did he think a member of his own family sabotaged his equipment? Is that what his misery was about?

"Talk about what happened to your scuba gear?"

His lips pinched as he looked over my shoulder, following something with his eyes. "Have you ever gotten involved in something maybe out of curiosity, or for the experience or whatever, or maybe just drifted into it out of ignorance, and had it turn out to be hard? Harder than you really wanted to deal with? Way harder?"

My relationship with Hal. "Yes."

"This is one of those things. And"—he frowned— "you'd have to promise to abide by certain decisions we make."

He did think it was a member of his family; he must. "If you're considering some quasi-tribal form of justice—"

He dropped my hands. "Look, I can't make you stay out of this. At least, I don't feel that would be fair. Not without your consent."

"I'm in it." I said so, and then wondered why. What did I care about McGuin's problems? I wasn't his lawyer. I wasn't anybody's lawyer. I was a hermit on extended leave, staying out of everybody's business including my own.

"Then you've got to promise." Determination hardened his features.

"Why?"

"Just promise. Please. Or stay out of it. It won't be fun."

"I'm a member of the state bar. With certain obligations to the system. I don't make blind promises."

"I guess I'm asking you to choose between being a lawyer and being . . ." He seemed at a loss. "Being a good person, I guess."

"The two things aren't mutually exclusive."

"I'm not saying they are, except sometimes, okay? This is one of those times." He sighed. "I'm going in. If you follow me, leave your obligations to the system out here. Just be you. If you don't want to do that, wait here and I'll be out in a few minutes with car keys."

When he walked away, I leaned on the hood of the Datsun. I closed my eyes, feeling cold and achy in the noontime wind. I could still see sparkling bubbles rising through kelp, still feel the snorkel in my mouth. I could feel McGuin's hand under mine on the throttle of the outboard.

Maybe my take on McGuin was dangerous: he seemed more real, more vital than anyone I'd encountered in a long while; than people who were truly part of my life.

I thought of Hal's parents and their polite manipulations, Hal's taciturn body at the far side of the bed.

I remembered McGuin holding his mother, begging her to talk to him. I remembered him with his aunt at the Clausens' house. Remembered his father talking about the family we choose.

Why was I so drawn to them? Just because they showed their pain? Just because they shared it, did something with it besides shut down, build walls, devise strategies?

Maybe I just needed to come out of the wind and see their fabric art again. See McGuin embrace his mother and beat his father at chess. Feel like a person, not a lawyer. Touch McGuin's energy after months of quiet co-existence with Hal.

Maybe I just wanted another experience. Wanted to swim

with McGuin's family as I'd swum with the otters, reassuring myself I could still try something new.

I glanced at the house and saw the curtains part, saw McGuin look out at me.

I wanted to be on his side of the curtain, that's all.

26

THE DINING ROOM table was laid with embroidered white cloth and a center runner of beveled mirror. It reflected candles in golden glass and lilies in a silver pitcher. Each of five places was set with fine goblets and antique china, mismatched. Salad plates were decorated with avocado, fennel, red pepper, and tiny dabs of gold and black caviar.

Lace sheers sent shadows flickering over the fabric art, catching highlights of brocade and lamé. But mostly the walls vanished, candles pooling light around the flowers. A votive at each place setting made the caviar glint like heaped bubbles.

Ted McGuin said, "I had them set a place for you."

I looked up at him, his skin glowing gold in the candlelight. I didn't know what to say. Though I'd dined with senators in their exquisite townhouses, this seemed an honor. The family's elegance was independent of wealth and therefore seemed more genuine, even valiant.

Behind McGuin, Hannah Arthur fretted over the salad plates, turning each so fennel topped it like a jaunty feather. A cigarette hung from her lips and she nodded distractedly to herself. Her red hair was tidily pinned and she wore a jacket resembling a Japanese kimono. When she looked up, her eyes caught the blue of the silk. She looked very young.

McGuin's mother stood beside her, watching me. Her face was serious, chin tucked down and eyes round in their deep sockets. She wore a shell-gray sweater that accented the soft beauty of her skin and brought out the drama of her gray-streaked hair.

Wyatt Lehommedieu looked the same as ever, shirt partly hitched out of his corduroys, smile friendly and intelligent and a little goofy, strawberry hair spilling over his high fore-head.

He rubbed his hands together. "I missed this."

I could smell the curries and chutneys to come. "Is it a special occasion?"

McGuin smiled wryly. "My aunt's a gourmet chef, and lunch is our meal."

"Food artiste." Hannah Arthur swept the cigarette from her lips, completing an arc with her kimonoed arm. "Yes, food. A sacrament, really. The only true ceremony left."

Lehommedieu grinned.

"I said *true* ceremony, buster! Not the licking of guru toes by—"

McGuin's mother made the smallest sound in the back of her throat. It was enough to silence her sister. Hannah looked deflated, in fact.

Lehommedieu explained, "Sarah's the latest addition to the communion."

"I thought you'd left the, um, communion. Are you going back?"

"Not to the community. But I never left the communion."

"Just don't get greedy about my sister!" Hannah's ciga-rette was back between her lips, her words a hard-bitten mut-ter. "We're Siamese twins, born in different years. So."

"Let's sit down," Sarah suggested.

McGuin guided me to one of two chairs facing a cabinet with a curved glass door. It was filled with small treasures of cut crystal. Candlelight danced in their sharp etchings. McGuin sat beside me and Lehommedieu sat opposite, the women at the ends of the table.

I watched McGuin, feeling suddenly shy. I wanted to un-

fold my embroidered napkin, pick up my silver salad fork
when he did. Despite years of fast-lane luxury, I felt intimi-
dated in a house my aunt Diana would call shabby. Maybe
my elegance was merely purchased; maybe these people
would see that.

I could feel the dampness of my hair, smell the seawater.
I could still see McGuin floating unconscious in the kelp. It
made the caviar on my tongue seem absurd, the goblet in my
hand seem unreal. Candles in the daytime. McGuin beside
me. A red-haired black woman in a blue kimono.

Lehommedieu described his guru quoting another guru:
Attention is destiny. Hannah said, No, no, more often lack
of attention—drifting along—is destiny. Drifting, Sarah corrected, is a way of surrendering, of capitulating to attention.
And the family boiled into dispute about whether it was possible or desirable to "transcend your attention."

I drank white wine. I tried to visualize my family, my
associates debating anything so nonmaterial.

Chutneys and cold meats came next. Curried rice and
glazed baby carrots. There wasn't much: a scant lunch for
four divided by five. But the presentation more than com-
pensated.

Hannah seemed to hear my thought. "That's the pleasure
of it, that it's really not much, really so ordinary. Like Sarah's
art—dull little scraps of fabric. But put them together . . ."

Lehommedieu, still flushed from passionate polemics,
said, "But that's it! You've hit on the essence of communion—the ordinary made extraordinary by union."

"Where's the creativity in that?" Hannah scoffed. "You're
just the clay, the scraps. Not the artist."

"That's the magic of it." Sarah's voice was faint. She
stared at her dinner plate. "To be a tiny piece of velveteen
that knows its importance."

"As the eye skips over it."

"Not the discerning eye. It takes faith to understand there
would be a hole without you."

I folded my napkin, feeling my head bow, my eyes fill
with tears. It was the calmness of it, I think, after so much
novelty and stress. I'd found a safe place to be scared. The
thought of Hal seized me like a cramp.

I sat with McGuin while the others cleared the table. I realized I hadn't talked during the meal, hadn't even complimented the food.

I tried to do that now. I glanced at McGuin and couldn't seem to speak.

He moved his chair closer to mine, taking my hand in both of his. He lowered his forehead so that he looked up at me, white showing beneath the pupils of his eyes.

"In a few minutes, Ricky Clausen will be here. We called him before you came in."

I was surprised. "He didn't seem friendly toward you."

"No." He raised his brows. "He's been trying to kill me."

I shook my head.

"I taught him the techniques myself. I taught him that sodium ignites when it comes in contact with water—that's how he capsized my dinghy, it has to be. By encasing sodium in gelatin and taping it to the pontoons."

Lehommedieu reentered the room carrying a decanter of what looked like port. "He must have spritzed gasoline vapor into the dinghy's air valves."

McGuin nodded. "Probably took a garden vaporizer and poured some gas in it—we've done that a couple of times. Inflated balloons with a little vapor and popped them with sparklers taped to sticks. Vwoosh." He looked sheepish. "Once the gelatin melted—time it for maybe half an hour's submersion—and the sodium touched water . . ." He shook his head slowly. "It would burn through the rubber and ignite the gas vapor in the pontoons."

"Which would send a flume of fire and smoke out the hole, pulling the air out for a fast collapse." Lehommedieu put down the decanter, reaching into the cabinet for dessert wineglasses. "Funny we didn't think of Ricky."

"Mom did."

"When you told me and Hannah last night, it made perfect sense. We must have realized, on some level. It wasn't a shock. Just sad."

"He's a bright kid, and we've done a lot of fooling with chemicals." McGuin sat straight, head bent, staring at my fingers, which he absentmindedly manipulated. "He pockets stuff from his high school chem lab; used to bring it here, show off what he'd learned, see if I knew any tricks."

Both men looked tired, incipient pouches beneath their eyes.

"When did you realize?" I wondered.

"The thing with the superglue was so unsophisticated I didn't suspect Ricky. It must have been an afterthought, maybe when he rigged the boat."

Lehommedieu poured three ports, handing one to me and one to McGuin.

McGuin continued, "After the boat, I knew."

"You almost drowned. Twice." My voice was tight with fear. With the memory of McGuin on the surface, mouth plugged with rubber and seawater washing over his nose.

"I'd call it fifty-fifty." He released my hand, looking at his father. "Good solid plans with a fifty-fifty chance of working."

He sounded so matter-of-fact. It angered me. "You could have—"

"I'm a strong swimmer and there was no telling where I'd be with the boat. At least a fifty-fifty chance of getting back to shore."

"The scuba gear—"

"All I'd have to do is get myself back up to the surface. I'm an experienced diver."

Lehommedieu reached across the table, squeezing his son's hand.

Sarah and Hannah returned to their chairs. Lehommedieu blinked away tears, releasing McGuin's hand so he could fill their glasses.

"It could have worked." My horror seemed to eclipse theirs, but then, they'd had time to assimilate this.

I looked around the table. "He could be dead now."

Sarah stared at the candles. Hannah drank her port quickly, reaching for the decanter.

"Will you have Ricky arrested?"

I remembered how uncommunicative McGuin had been after his boat capsized, telling the police he remembered nothing. I remembered him tossing an important piece of evidence over the side of the motorboat this morning. This was why he'd sworn me to secrecy: the answer was no, he didn't want the police involved.

"He could try again," I pointed out. "This fifty-fifty stuff—those aren't good odds, not repeatedly. Jesus."

Sarah's voice was sharp. "He'll stop."

"You've got to call the police," I insisted. "You have no authority over this boy. No way to force him into counseling even, not unless you can persuade his family—"

"They won't listen to us," McGuin said simply. "If we told them this, they'd just—"

"Those awful, awful people!" His aunt lit a shaky cigarette. "Oh no. No. They'd never believe. They'd call us names and tie the blinders on tighter."

"If you present it as a necessity for the boy's mental health—"

"They still wouldn't believe it," McGuin rubbed his eyes. "That's the nature of their feelings about us. Going to them is not even an option."

"Put a threat behind it. Tell them you'll call the police if they don't arrange treatment."

His hand dropped. "They wouldn't believe that either. Ricky wouldn't. He'd know it was an empty threat. Fuck—after all the chess games, all the Mr. Wizard stuff we've done together. No way."

Sarah summed up. "We have no authority to help him. And the people who do won't."

I wanted to shake McGuin. "You can't just go along hoping you'll survive his booby traps."

He raised his brows. "No. I've shown him some pretty out-there stuff. He could blow up my house, if he wanted to."

Sarah's head sank slowly toward her folded forearms. McGuin put his hand on her shoulder.

"Call the police, McGuin." I pressed my fingers into his knee. "You've got to. You tried to protect Karen, and look what happened: she got crazier. You can't protect people from the consequences—"

"Don't." McGuin's tone was stern. "Don't compare this to Karen. I don't have the power to help Ricky—not in the sense of committing him. And as far as his family's concerned, I don't have the—''

"Right skin color," his aunt interrupted.

"—credibility to persuade them. And I'm fucking not turning him over to the cops. What do you think they'd do?''

"He's only fifteen. He'd be arrested as a juvenile."

"On what charge?'' His voice was grim.

"Attempted murder. Probably."

"What good would it do? Say he got a light sentence—till he was seventeen? Would that be considered a light sentence?''

"Yes.'' If the charges against him were proved, it would be unusually light. The crimes were premeditated, in spite of the sick passion fueling them.

"Do you think two years in prison would help a fifteen-year-old kid?'' McGuin's skin color deepened as his brows sank into a frown. "Would you do that to a child you've been close to? Could you? Could you stand to think of him at the mercy of streetwise gang members? Bad-tempered guards? After what he's been through already?''

McGuin felt guilty about Karen, felt he'd killed her. Blamed himself for her nephew's madness. It was in his voice.

"He said Karen was the only one in the family who loved him,'' Hannah recalled. Her eyes glowed with tears. "He's a very smart boy, you see; smart enough to know that all their doting means nothing, really. That all he has to do is grow his hair too long or get bad grades or date a black girl—''

"They'd turn on him like that,'' McGuin agreed.

I recalled the Clausens' comments about their daughter: that she'd been beautiful and liked nice clothes once, that she'd gotten good grades and made them proud. But they'd abandoned her for marrying McGuin.

It was something an astute boy would notice.

"The fact remains,'' I felt like a cold-hearted interloper, "if you do nothing, then nothing is done for him. If you have him arrested, at least he gets treatment.''

"He gets jail.'' McGuin tossed his napkin onto the table. "I wouldn't do that to Ricky.''

"If he hates you enough to try to kill you, do you really

think talking to him—if that's your plan—is going to do any good?''

"Do I have any other option? Realistically?"

"Talk to his family."

"It won't work. Guaranteed."

"Then you have no choice: let the state step in." I looked around the table. "You didn't see your son today—he almost drowned. I almost watched him die."

I heard Lehommedieu say something, maybe something meant to soothe me.

"This Ricky is crazy." My voice spiraled in pitch. "He's crazy and you're talking about trying to—what?—do for him in one conversation what a psychiatrist would take years doing! You're not magicians! Believe me, I've known crazy people! I've gotten them acquitted—" I caught my breath. There was no room here for my baggage.

McGuin put both elbows on the table, hiding behind his palms. His mother, still rounded over her forearms, shook with silent tears. Hannah reached out to Lehommedieu and he slid to his knees, walking to her like Porgy to Bess.

Somewhere in the house a clock ticked. The silence stretched long, at wild odds with my anger and frustration.

I couldn't keep silent about this: I wouldn't. Damn my promise to McGuin.

Yes, they'd been close to Ricky Clausen, and jail was a harsh alternative. But so was untreated madness—of all people, they should know that. Of all people, Karen McGuin's husband should know that.

If they didn't do something more than talk—*talk*, for Christ's sake—to a boy who'd tried three times—

I found I was shaking. I scooted my chair farther from the table. Couldn't get the images out of my head: McGuin swimming crazy circles in the surf as his body temperature plunged. McGuin floating on his scuba tank, mouth plugged and nose filled with seawater.

I had no emotional attachment to Ricky Clausen; that was a good thing. I would be here when he arrived. (What had they said to make him come? That they knew? That they'd call the cops if he didn't?) I would listen, I would watch.

And when their talk failed in its objective, as it surely

would—as any unbiased person must know it would—then I'd do what I thought best. To hell with promises to the contrary.

I looked at Ted McGuin, rubbing his forehead with his fingers, and I knew I'd do whatever it took to protect him.

When the doorbell rang, Hannah cried out. Sarah sat straight, shivering as if dunked in ice water.

McGuin rose and left the room. I hurried after him. The boy might have a gun, a knife.

I was right behind him when he opened the door.

27

Sandy slouched against a porch support, looking pale and puffy-eyed, still sick from yesterday's knock on the head.

"Hoping you were here," he drawled. "Worried when I saw your car at McGuin's and the boat gone. I was thinking you must have taken McGuin along to pilot." He smiled at McGuin. "Sorry to just drop in. I thought maybe you'd come here to pick up your aunt's car, drive yourselves back. Just a little worried."

"He hit Sandy!" I grabbed McGuin's arm. "You're not the only one. You've got to call the—"

"He must have been in the shed rigging the regulator." McGuin didn't look at me. "It was just panic, probably. Just wanting to get away."

He seemed determined to believe Ricky posed no danger to others. Determined to find limits to the boy's madness.

Sandy stepped past him, wrapping a long arm around my shoulder. "What happened to your hair? You okay? What's going on?"

McGuin wheeled on me. "Don't! Please."

I felt Sandy's arm tighten around me. "What the hell—?"

McGuin stood almost eye to eye with me. I could smell

the sea salt on his skin. I could almost feel the warmth of his body. ''Please don't say any more. Family business—at least for now. Please.''

What was it Jerry Clausen had scoffed? That ''jigs'' always put their business in the street?

I looked at Sandy. Years of trust, of working together, of knowing he was beside me, with me.

''Please,'' McGuin urged.

I reached both hands up, touching McGuin's shoulders. And McGuin pulled me close, wrapping his big arms around me.

When I caught my breath, when we let go of one another, I turned guiltily back to Sandy, found him staring slack-jawed and ghostly white. He looked at me like I'd slapped him.

I guess maybe I had.

''Sandy.'' I didn't know what to say. He'd been attacked by Ricky Clausen; he had a right to know. And he was my partner, my best friend; he had strong claims on my allegiance.

Sarah appeared in the entryway. She walked rigidly, hand held to her heart. When she saw Sandy at the door, she leaned heavily against a wall.

They had so much to fear. They'd been through so much already. I looked at her, looked at Sandy.

I didn't know what to do.

I looked at Ted McGuin (wished I could do nothing but look at him). He mouthed the word, ''Please.''

I was almost grateful to hear a screech of bicycle tires, a clatter of falling metal on concrete. I was almost glad to see Ricky Clausen heave himself from the sidewalk where he'd spilled. I was almost glad to see him in the walkway, red-faced, hands at his hips like a gunfighter.

Glad until I saw the unallayed torment on McGuin's face. Until I saw Sarah surge toward the door, arms out as if aching to embrace the boy.

Ricky stood frozen, tensed into a cramped, unnatural stance. His face was glazed with sweat. His shirt was stained under the arms and in the hollow of the chest. His black hair was plastered damply to his forehead.

Watching him, it was much harder to take the uncompromising view. He didn't look like a crazy saboteur. He looked like a wildly miserable teenage boy. But then, I supposed he was both.

He opened and closed his mouth several times, waving his arm in a "back off" gesture that stopped Sarah midstride. Her arms shrank to her sides and her spine wilted. She turned, cowering against the doorframe as if seeking sanctuary.

McGuin stepped past her, hurrying down the walkway.

Ricky backed away, teeth bared and eyes scrunched with unshed tears.

McGuin, shorter but far wider than the boy, encased him in a powerful embrace.

At first Ricky was rigid, enduring the contact with a look of anguished horror. McGuin's head burrowed into the boy's collarbone as if desperate for succor.

Then Ricky barraged McGuin with flaying fists and appalled grunts. He looked like he was trying to beat off some startling insect. McGuin continued clinging as Ricky's panic sent them dancing across the untended grass. When one of them stumbled, both went down with an audible emptying of lungs.

And then Sandy was on top of them, pulling them apart with limb-bending techniques learned on the L.A. police force.

"What the hell?" he muttered. "Come on kid. Come on. What's this going to solve, huh? McGuin, back off. Kid needs space, all right?"

Hannah rushed to the tangle of men. She dropped to her knees. Her fingers found Ricky Clausen's cheeks, touching them as if sculpting him from clay. Jesus Christ, he'd almost killed her nephew.

He stared at her as if at some monster. Maybe I did too.

"What's he doing here?" Sandy demanded of McGuin. "What's going on?"

Ricky slapped Hannah's hands away.

"Come on, kid. We'll give you a lift home. Put your bike in the trunk." Sandy looked over his shoulder at me. A signal to do what? Support him in his effort to break this up?

Behind me in the entryway, Lehommedieu spoke quiet words to Sarah, coaxing her back indoors. On the grass,

McGuin stared at Ricky, who scooted backward away from him.

I knew the family needed its opportunity to speak to Ricky, needed to believe they'd done their best to reclaim him. I didn't think it would help; I did know that to them it was paramount.

How could I make Sandy understand?

I couldn't reveal the family's agenda, or the reasons for it. Sandy, with his clients to consider and his professional reputation at stake, would deal with this in a way bound to involve the authorities.

I was torn, paralyzed in the doorway as Sandy looked to me for support. Looked to me to help him hustle Ricky Clausen into his car and out of this situation.

In that moment of indecision, I watched them; McGuin's expression of petition and apprehension. His aunt's sudden, shattering pessimism. Ricky's crawling-away horror.

The discussion couldn't happen in Sandy's presence, not unless I broke McGuin's confidence.

My alternative was to get Sandy away from here, leaving Ricky to McGuin's entreaties and explanations.

Except that the boy looked feral in his distress. I'd seen that look on clients' faces, seen how bestial madness could be. I had to stay. The family needed someone objective—someone who didn't love Ricky Clausen—with them to monitor, to warn.

From the house across the street came the shout, "You people need held? Should I phone nine one one?"

I ran down the porch steps, calling, "No. We're fine." When I reached Sandy, I said, "Help us get Clausen inside. Let's not do this out here."

"Home would be a better idea," Sandy said coolly.

"No. There's a reason. Please, everyone get up and go in. The neighbors."

McGuin was the first on his feet, bending to hook a forearm under Ricky's armpit.

"Sandy, please. Trust me."

He blinked at me dubiously, then took hold of Clausen's other arm.

The two men lifted the boy easily; he seemed too surprised to resist.

Several awkward, weaving steps took the group inside. I shut the door behind us, noticing Sarah and Wyatt sitting cross-legged, forehead to forehead, on the living room floor. He was speaking quietly, his hands on his wife's shoulders. Her eyes were shut tight as she listened.

McGuin said, "The couch," and the men deposited Ricky Clausen on its threadbare velvet.

Ricky flattened as if trying to back through it. His face was white and clammy now: flight, not fight.

McGuin scowled at Sandy, obviously wishing him gone. He looked at me, hoping I would make that happen.

I didn't know what else to do: "Ricky's been booby-trapping McGuin's scuba equipment. He's the one who sabotaged the boat."

McGuin mouthed the words "Oh God."

Hannah cried out, "Oh!"

"They don't want the police involved. They just want him to get help." I grabbed Sandy's arm. "Let's give them a chance. Give them room to talk."

"But if the kid really—"

"They realize that." I tugged at Sandy's arm, so thin and familiar. "Give them a chance."

Ricky's head was pressed so deeply into the couch it looked painful. His eyes were wide and dilated. His expression said, *They know.*

"Sandy!" I pulled him away from the couch, into the corner behind Lehommedieu. I planted myself in front of him.

Ted McGuin dropped to his knees, staring at his nephew-in-law. "I'm sorry," he said. "I'm sorry about the gun. I fucked up—I was trying to help her, get her to choose to be alive."

Anger lashed Ricky's features. "Choose? You told her what to choose—a bullet in the head so you wouldn't have to look at her anymore!"

"No. No." McGuin shook his head ferociously. "That's not what I wanted. I wanted her to get over it. Choose to get over it."

"Get over it!" The boy's voice cracked. "She was sick. You don't get over being sick 'cause someone pressures you! Anyway, I don't want to discuss her with you!"

Hannah stood behind him, fumbling in her kimono pockets. "Oh but we must, you see, we really, really must."

I could feel Sandy tense behind me. He'd already heard enough to fry McGuin: heard him admit giving his wife the gun, lying to the D.A. about it.

"I don't have to talk about my aunt with you guys! You pretended you were such hot shit to her, but she wasn't craz— she wasn't unhappy before she met you! She never would have killed herself! I don't know what you did to make her feel like that, but I don't have to talk to you about her! You don't even deserve me talking to you!" Ricky's voice was loud and shrill, his face contorted.

"We really . . . loved her." McGuin's eyelids drooped, his voice was slow and quiet. He seemed to be shutting down, as if the level of hostility was too much for him.

Hadn't he known the boy would blame him not only for his aunt's death but for her mental illness? Hadn't he known, given the attempts to murder him, how big the problem was?

McGuin folded, arms curling around his face.

I stepped past Lehommedieu. "Ricky, look: He thought he'd given your aunt too much space to work things out. He'd left her alone, which is what she said she wanted. Then she tried to kill herself. And he blamed himself for not forcing her—dragging her, really—into counseling. So—"

"So he gave her a fucking gun?" Ricky leaped to his feet. "When I went over there, she was holding it on her cheek—"

He clapped his hand over his mouth. His eyes widened. A sound rumbled up his throat; it might have been some animal moaning in its lair. He reached out a long arm, the smell of sweat souring the air.

He bolted from the room.

I heard Sandy shout, "Damn!" and felt a rush of air as he pursued the boy.

From the yard came a clatter, the bark of raised voices. Inside, a staccato of *Ohs* from Hannah.

I reached the door behind Lehommedieu, in time to see

Sandy push Ricky into the passenger seat of his rented Nissan. He slammed the door, glaring at me as he straightened.

Lehommedieu and I stood there in breathless worry, doing nothing. Nothing seemed appropriate.

Sandy crossed to the driver's side and climbed in.

"He has a way of making people confide in him." I sounded hoarse, unsure. We watched the car pull away from the curb. "It might be good. Good for Ricky. Less charged than talking to you guys at this point."

But Sandy had no stake in seeing things resolved as this family wished. If anything, his sympathies were with the Clausens. He'd want to tuck the boy into his "natural" nest.

I followed Lehommedieu back inside. McGuin was standing now, breathing hard. His mother was behind him, hands on his chest, forehead on his back.

Maybe Sandy was right: maybe it was better for Ricky Clausen to return to his family. What could these people do for him? His wounds were too deep; maybe theirs were too.

"We could have him watched." I wanted to console them. "Until he's not so angry, not so crazy. Keep a tail on him until he calms down. Until you can talk to him."

Now that I'd seen Ricky again, so gangly and young, I couldn't imagine calling the police.

"Have him watched for a while." My tone wheedled, infected with McGuin's quixotic denial.

McGuin's face was pensive now. "What did he mean, 'when I went there'?" He turned to his mother. "Was he saying he saw Karen the day she—"

Sarah put her fingers on his lips. "Yes." She nodded emphatically. "That's what I heard."

"He could have meant—"

Lehommedieu interrupted. "Our impressions at the time are going to be more valid than picking apart the words now."

"If he was there that day, why didn't he mention it before? If he saw her with the gun—"

"Ted." Sarah's expression matched his. In troubled reflection, their resemblance was startling. "He might have dropped in on Karen. Or phoned and heard the message. Reached her just as . . ."

"You do know"—maybe this wasn't the time for me to

offer the sheriff's observation—"that the gun was several inches from Karen's face when it went off?"

Hannah made a choking sound, turning away.

McGuin stared at me as if I'd spoken Chinese.

"If Ricky saw Karen with the gun to her cheek," I continued, "he'd certainly rush over and pull her arm back. Which would account for the gun being so far away. If he tried to stop her . . ."

Sarah put her hands on McGuin's cheeks. "Then he would truly have to hate you, Ted. Because if he stopped hating you for a minute, he might have to blame himself."

"Yes," I agreed. "For not getting the gun away. Not keeping it from firing."

Sarah buried her face in McGuin's chest. Her voice was muffled. "He would have to blame you with all his ingenuity and all his passion."

"Or he'd have to blame himself." McGuin spoke as if repeating a lesson.

Sarah looked up at him, eyes glistening. "And that must be unbearable."

28

McGuin said, "I'm taking your car." When he received no reply, he put his hands over Sarah's, gently removing them from his cheeks. "Mom? Car keys?"

She blinked as if trying to understand the request, so shockingly ordinary.

Lehommedieu stepped up to them, digging in his pocket. He handed McGuin a key ring. "Do you want us along?"

"No." Emphatically.

"Just me?" Lehommedieu's voice seemed carefully flat; no way of telling if he was asking to go or merely making himself available.

Again McGuin said, "No." He glanced at me.

"I'm coming," I told him.

I didn't care if he wanted me along.

But he looked glad.

Goodbyes seemed superfluous. We walked out.

We climbed into the family's Datsun. I rolled the window down halfway, as far as it would go, and closed the overflowing ashtray. The stench of tobacco clung to matted sheepskin seat covers.

McGuin put the car in gear and pulled away. I sneaked a

glance at his profile. Couldn't remember the last time I'd had to fight to keep from touching someone. I stared out the passenger window.

We drove to a house I'd never seen before, a modest ranch-style on a street of new ranch-styles: Ricky's house. Sandy's car wasn't there.

McGuin hesitated, then swung out of the car. He pounded on Mark Clausen's door. Half a minute later, he pounded again, peering through a glass panel. Then he walked around the side of the house to the back, returning a few minutes later.

I'd opened the car door by then, gasping for air that didn't stink of ashtray.

McGuin looked dispirited. "Mark doesn't like me much— I guess out of loyalty to his mother. But he probably would have talked to me. I know *they* won't."

We drove in silence to the Clausen's larger version of their son's house. There was no sign of Sandy's car.

"He's not here." McGuin sounded both disappointed and relieved.

"Sandy might have taken him to a restaurant or some-place."

He shook his head, staring at the house. "Ricky's too upset. They'd want privacy."

"Sandy's good with people." I put a reassuring hand on McGuin's bicep.

He turned to me, and we locked together.

A minute later, we unclenched. Jerry Clausen had flung open his front door. Easter egg polyesters didn't soften his attitude of menace. Both his hands were wrapped around a baseball bat. He looked McGuin in the eye and raised the bat to waist level.

McGuin watched him, shoulders hunching.

Clausen took a furious step onto the porch, waving the bat. His wife stood behind him, gesturing operatically as she spoke to him.

McGuin started the car. "Your house," he said.

"Probably." Acres of land to tramp; Sandy and Ricky would certainly find privacy there. Sandy would think of it: a place to calm the boy before taking him home.

McGuin pulled away, frowning into the rearview mirror.

We backtracked to the highway dissecting Hillsdale. I melted into the tobacco cloud of sheepskin, muscles in my calves aching from this morning's heavy fins. I watched the town fly by, then the dairy hills and redwoods. I tried not to think.

As soon as we turned onto the road leading to my house, we spotted Sandy's Nissan. Before we parked, Hal stepped out of the cabin, rangy in his jeans and boots, a V-neck sweater pulled over his bare chest.

I felt my stomach cramp. We went back a long way. As long as I could remember. I knew every line of his face, every nuance of his touch.

But I could still feel McGuin's arms around me. My skin still danced from the pressure of his fingers.

I climbed out of the car. The task at hand: "Hi. Did Sandy bring Ricky Clausen here?"

Hal frowned, cheeks stubbled and hollow, thick brows lowered so that his eyes were cast in shadow. He regarded McGuin, spoke distractedly.

"They headed down to the creek."

"Okay." I stood beside the car, conscious of McGuin climbing out. I felt hot in the afternoon wind.

"You been swimming?"

I touched my hair. It had dried stiff with salt, must look awful. "We took the boat back. I tried out"—I hesitated over the name—"Ted's snorkel."

Hal folded his arms across his chest. He leaned on a porch support, watching me.

Here it was: the relationship in microcosm. He stood his ground and I stood mine. Maybe we both seethed with needs and wishes and fears and explanations. But neither of us offered any. Neither of us crossed the yard.

I wanted to say, Hal, I'm tired of us. I'm tired of how we are together, and I have no faith in our ability to change, not when the pattern is so encoded.

The relationship is maimed. Here's a gun. Choose it or kill it.

I stood beside the car. Hal stood on the porch.

McGuin said, "Take me down to the creek? Or point me in the right direction?"

I told Hal, "I'll be back in a while."

Hal nodded and went inside.

I walked swiftly away, eyes blind with tears. McGuin was beside me. We hurried.

In less than five minutes, we stood at the crest of the gorge, looking down the tangled embankment at the creek below. It sparkled with sunlight, benign without its characteristic shroud of fog and dapple of rain. Small waterfalls poured serenely over the rocks.

And suddenly Sandy came into view. He was on the other side of the gorge, the steep side. I supposed he'd walked north along the woods trail, crossing where the stream met meadow, where Hal and I had piled rocks for easy-hike days, days when his right leg wouldn't take him up embankments.

Sandy's anorak was visible as movement between trunks of redwood and spruce. A moment later, a light-colored shirt stood out beside him. Ricky Clausen was with him, looking down at the creek. From a hundred yards away, he looked like a doll: thin, tall, stiff-armed.

He and Sandy stood together, maybe talking, maybe not. Neither moved.

Then Sandy made a visor of his hand, scanning the opposite crest. When he spotted us, he took a large step backward. Clausen turned his back on the creek to face him.

McGuin sounded tense. "Quickest way to get over?"

"Getting down is easy. Getting up the other side is tricky. If we go around the way they probably went, it'll take ten, fifteen minutes longer."

"No. Show me where to climb."

I started down the embankment. Felt his arm on my shoulder. "You don't have to come. Just point it out."

I looked over my shoulder. Such an unusual face. "I want to go. Easier than explaining."

I continued down, testing the hillside for tree root footholds. The ground was drier than usual, surer underfoot. I moved confidently, clinging to fir saplings and thick stalks of yarrow. At least I'd learned to do this. I vowed not to let the Bankruptcy Code become the focus of my life. Not again.

Two thirds of the way down, surrounded by ferns and giant horsetails, I looked up the other side. The men weren't there anymore. Had Ricky seen us? Insisted they go back the way they'd come? Had Sandy led him away, hoping to avoid another scene?

I'd never forded the creek without my rubber boots. I quickly catalogued rocks and fallen trees, knowing there was no way to keep our shoes dry. The smell of mud and skunk cabbage filled the air.

McGuin stepped into the rushing water, balancing on submerged rocks to keep himself ankle-deep rather than knee-deep. He crossed gracefully, quickly; a bulky man used to activity, used to traversing unusual spaces.

The gorge was concave on the far side, most easily climbable where slides had piled rocks and tree limbs, exposing foothold roots among the slick ferns.

I led us to the best spot, and we started up. I was conscious of a certain pride. I might be awkward in a wet suit, but I could do this. And McGuin had never seen my real forte, never seen me with a jury.

My stomach knotted. What made me think he ever would?

We stopped when we reached the top, stood there breathing hard, listening to the rush of water, the squawk of jays, the creak of trees. The wind brought the smell of redwood needles and sun-warmed spruce.

Sandy stomped out of a stand of trees, hands in his anorak pockets. He stopped when he saw us. "Fuck! Fuck a mother-loving duck!" His expression was as cross as his words.

McGuin turned, apparently ready to fight: elbows out, knees slightly bent.

Sandy stepped closer. "He took off like a fucking antelope—Jesus, that kid's fast."

"Which way?" McGuin's voice jerked with impatience.

Sandy pointed in the direction from which he'd come, and McGuin was off.

When I tried to follow, Sandy grabbed my arm, nearly yanking me off balance. "What the hell gives?"

He glowered down at me, shucking every vestige of Gary Cooper pleasantness.

"Find him," I urged. "Let's go."

"Why?"

"You heard—he was there when his aunt killed herself! He's been trying to kill McGuin! He needs help." I pulled my arm free.

"Not from McGuin."

"Well, he's not going to get it from the Clausens!"

"Stands a hell of a better chance with his own family than he does with a bunch of—"

"What? A bunch of what?" I felt my hands lock into fists.

Sandy grabbed my shoulders as if to shake me. "He doesn't belong with those people, don't you get it?"

"A bunch of what?"

"Head in the clouds, unrealistic—"

"They're artists!"

"Artists, my ass! People won't work hard and stand on their own feet!" His face was dark with anger. "They act like the Clausens are shit. Why? Because they work for a living and do what they feel it's right for people to do—keep a comfortable roof over their kids' heads, be proud of them for doing good in school, encouraging behavior that keeps this society together." He shook me. "What the hell's wrong with that? Who's being narrow-minded? That redhead goes over there picking at their wounds, acting superior because she's got swear words on her T-shirt and they're not artists, they're regular people. Well, baby, it ain't easy being regular! And they're the ones got rejected after a whole life of loving their daughter! You think Karen picked McGuin for his fucking brains? No, she had it in for her parents, that's what—"

"What do you know about McGuin?" I shoved him away. "What do you know about his brains? You haven't even talked to him!"

"He's a Goddamn kid! Might as well get wet for Ricky Clausen!"

My arm sprang back as if it had a life of its own. Snapped forward and cracked Sandy's jaw.

He staggered back a step, touching his cheek. "What the hell is it with you? Di Palma's not bad enough? Not enough of a social liability? You got to go after someone even more screwed up?"

I felt chilled through. Had I really slapped Sandy?

Chilled through, really hearing him now: How could you prefer these men to me? His defense of the Clausens: What do you have against normal, decent people? Former cop, traditional guy, Sandy Arkelett. Oh God.

He backed away, face flushed. Turned and disappeared into the woods.

I stood there shaking. Doubled over and tried to think. What now? What was important? Find McGuin and Clausen? Go after Sandy? Turn around and go home, talk to Hal?

Twigs snapped behind me. I straightened. Not Sandy—he'd gone the other way.

I turned to find Ricky Clausen watching me, panting, hand clamped to his side as if quelling a stitch.

I swallowed, tried to calm down. "Easy to go in circles out here. Want me to walk you back?"

He blinked rapidly, lower lip throbbing with tics. "I don't know."

"Why did you leave Sandy?"

"Sick of—" His mouth clamped for a moment. "Sick of talking. What's his problem? My dad hire him to tell me how great my family is?"

"Everyone's trying to think of a way to deal with you, I guess. Sandy thinks your family will get you through this."

He looked sullenly at the ground.

"And Ted's family wants you back. They love you and they want to try to help you."

His head snapped up, eyes crackling with anger and revulsion. Clearly that was not an acceptable option.

Behind him, McGuin moved stealthily toward us, his head down like a jungle cat.

"I gather you went to your aunt's house the day she— I'm sorry you had to see that—see her kill—"

He turned away. Blind, angry paces brought him into near collision with McGuin.

When he became aware of it, his arms jerked like a marionette's. He became a catapult of fists. McGuin took them in the torso, the side of the head, the face. Then he closed in, wrapping both arms around Ricky, holding him in a staggering dance as the boy struggled himself closer to exhaustion.

It was hell to watch. Jays screamed in the trees. Hot dust and humus swirled in the air.

The two of them fell, rolling on twigs and pine needles. I heard a thump of fist on flesh, and suddenly Ricky was scrambling away. McGuin curled up, eyes squeezed shut and lips drawn away from his teeth.

Ricky backed away, his arms flapping. "How did it feel to watch her do it? How did it feel?" The words were rapid and staccato, as if he fired them. "Show you," he said. "Show you."

And he ran to the crest of the gorge.

I took a horrified step forward. Out of the corner of my eye, I saw McGuin surge to his knees.

We were far too slow.

Ricky Clausen arched his back and tipped forward as if diving into a pool.

And he was gone. Right off the embankment. Gone.

Birds took wing. I saw their shadows over the creek when I looked down.

I almost didn't stop in time. A vertiginous unreality almost carried me a step too far.

I looked down and saw the fluttering bird shadows. I saw Ricky Clausen's body.

He'd landed facedown, legs at impossible angles.

I stood there paralyzed. I'd have stood there forever, that's how I felt. I'd have stood in frozen denial, I don't know how long.

Right away, Ted McGuin began sliding and clawing his way down the gorge. Before I could make myself believe it had happened, he was halfway down the bank.

By the time McGuin reached the creek, Sandy was beside me, asking questions.

I watched McGuin lope into the water, clutching one leg as if he'd hurt it. I watched him kneel in the water beside Ricky, sliding his fingers under the boy's face and gently raising it partway out of the stream. I watched him bend close, ear to Ricky's mouth. I expected him to turn the boy over, pull him from the creek perhaps. Instead, he lay close to him, hand still under his cheek.

"Laura!" Sandy's voice was shrill from repetition. "What happened?"

Water pouring over him, McGuin began blowing into Ricky's mouth.

By the time I turned to Sandy, he too was clambering down the impossible side of the gorge.

My limbs felt heavy. I couldn't seem to think.

I should do something. I began to run. Hardly thinking, hardly breathing, I went the long way around. I lacked coordination to tackle the embankment now, I knew that.

I ran. Still, it seemed forever before I reached the cabin.

I stumbled in and dialed 911. I begged them to hurry.

It didn't occur to me to call out for Hal. It didn't occur to me to seek him out for help or consolation.

I went outside to wait for the ambulance.

29

T ED MCGUIN CAME out of the emergency room wearing teal scrubs, his skin an ashen beige, his eyes red-rimmed after a long night. I stepped up hastily, partially blocking him from the Clausens' hostile stares. He glanced over my shoulder, years of hurt in the pinched way he averted his eyes.

Sandy sat with the Clausens, sat like a statue, not looking at me. I'd talked to them briefly, many hours earlier, explaining what had happened. I didn't tell them McGuin's resuscitation had saved Ricky. They blamed him so completely. What was the use?

"The doc's coming out in a minute to talk to them," McGuin said. "They don't want to hear it from me."

"No."

"It could be a lot worse. A lot. Broken bones are nothing. Spinal damage—that would be a drag."

I could hear the hush as the Clausens strained to listen, needing information.

McGuin raised his voice. "There probably won't be permanent deficits. He's young, and with luck everything will mend."

I heard Ricky's grandmother sob. A grumble from her husband.

"When he stabilizes, they'll take him to intensive care." A long sigh. "And then to M.H.U."

The mental health unit for involuntary commitment: standard after a suicide attempt. So much for the state not stepping in.

"But that's good," I said quietly. "He'll get help."

McGuin looked pessimistic. "I've taken kids over there. They see all that safety glass, all the locked doors. Their knees literally give out. They double over, throwing up—the response is that visceral."

"Help's more important than setting." I said it, but I knew it was bullshit. "Treatment" hadn't helped my client, Wallace Bean. He'd been as crazy as ever when he got out. And treatment hadn't helped Karen Clausen either, not for long.

I changed the subject. "Did you call your family?"

"No." Another pained glance at the Clausens. "This is going to be hard for them. I thought I'd tell them in person."

"Do you want me to go with you?"

The question hung there for a moment; I wanted to cower under its inappropriateness.

He said, "That would actually be very nice." He took my hand, gave it a quick squeeze. "I thought I'd wait until they transfer him to I.C.U."

I wondered what kind of hell it was watching doctors work on someone you loved.

"Would you meet me here in"—he shrugged—"three hours?"

"Yes. I'm going home till then. If you need me, call, okay?"

"Okay." A tentative smile.

I wished we weren't under the Clausens' scrutiny. Under Sandy's.

McGuin returned to the emergency room. I hesitated, considered leaving without explanation.

I walked to the nook that wasn't quite corridor and wasn't quite waiting room.

"Sandy?"

He rose, but made no move toward greater privacy. Beside him, the Clausens huddled: Mark with fierce arms around his mother, Jerry with fists clenched in his lap, the younger brother fiddling with a shoelace.

A wan, bearded doctor pushed through the emergency room door, striding toward the family.

I took Sandy's arm and walked him down the hall. The doctor began repeating what McGuin had told me.

"I'm going home for a while," I said. "Then I'm coming back here to pick Ted up."

Sandy's face was a study of composed distance. He looked like Hal. "Your life," he said.

"I'll see you later, I guess."

"Probably leave town in the morning. Talk to the D.A. first."

"I won't corroborate," I warned him.

It was simpler and cleaner this way. Because McGuin denied giving his wife the gun, the D.A. would not press charges.

"I'll tell the D.A. you misunderstood, Sandy."

He shrugged. "And to hell with the truth. Especially with an unaggressive—what did you call her?—cream puff of a D.A."

"Then why bother telling her?"

"It's my job."

"Will I see you soon?"

"Are you coming back to White, Sayres?"

I shook my head. "To practicing law, but not to Steve Sayres. Probably not to commercial law."

"Well. Legal community's pretty small. We're bound to cross paths."

He was about to turn away, go back to the Clausens.

"Sandy?"

"Yuh?"

"Just because I got close to McGuin? After all our—"

"Good times?" A long exhalation. "You really don't get it."

I tried to say "What?" but the word stuck in my throat.

"Listen," he said, "you go home, you ask Di Palma what

it was triggered that brain problem he had last year. Ask him to explain it to you, explain my part. Ask him to explain me.''

I watched him walk away, join the knot of grieving family.

Ask Hal to explain Sandy? That was no different from telling me I'd never understand. That was no different from telling me to ask the river.

But I'd get my answer one way or another. Soon, because the friendship meant a lot to me.

I knew where Sandy lived. And I was willing to meet him ninety-nine percent of the way.

I was almost out the door when Madeleine Abruzzi stepped into my path. We were both startled.

She laughed nervously.

''You're in uniform again.'' After so long a day, I could barely state the obvious.

''It goes in cycles. When we're busy, we tend to be very, very busy. Don't ask me why.'' The sheen of white nylon made her appear troglodyte pale, accentuating fine black hair above her lips and between her brows. ''I guess you heard about Ted McGuin's nephew-in-law.''

''Yes.''

She shook her head sourly. ''This really is too much— some of the nurses are complaining about having to work with him.''

''But he saved the boy's life.''

She turned her head, narrowing her eyes. *Don't be so naive,* her expression said. *You, a big city lawyer.* ''It's a little funny, all these suicide attempts around him.''

''What are you saying?'' I could hear the frost in my tone.

I guess she could too. ''I'm merely stating that it's odd. Extremely odd.''

''It was unlucky of him to marry into a family of depressives. I don't know that 'odd' is the right word.''

''Well, we'll never know how much of a hand he had in it, will we?''

With a barely civil smile, she continued down the hall.

It seemed no one hesitated to judge Ted McGuin. It must be easier than knowing him.

30

I OPENED THE door, surprised to find the cabin dark. It had been a long cab ride to McGuin's to pick up my car. A long ride home. Presumably Hal was in bed. I was a little annoyed he hadn't left a light on for me.

But then, it had been a while since we'd done small favors for each other. I wasn't good about that stuff. Neither was he.

Raised by the same people. Displaying the same defenses. Walls. Distance. Self-absorption.

How facile of me to want someone to save me from all that, to pull me like some frail damsel into a different reality.

I thought of the bobbing ocean, the glint of diving otters. The reflection of candlelight on a mirrored table.

I sat down in the dark. Nothing prevented me from changing reality on my own, I supposed. Taking Hal along for the ride.

I loved Hal. Maybe I was even addicted to him, to the feel of him and the smell of him, to quirky moods and attitudes I'd once found intriguing.

Would discussion make a difference? If we worked on the vocabulary, forced ourselves to knock the walls down?

And the answer came quickly: What about McGuin?

My skin came alive, and I felt a little cheap.

A hormone rush shouldn't keep me from working on a long-standing and very complicated relationship.

I rose from my chair. Damn.

I had a long history with Hal. I'd regret not giving it a chance.

I stood there shaking. I wasn't used to talking, not on any real level. I used words to get what I wanted. To hide what I didn't want to reveal and put a good spin on what I did.

I felt cold with apprehension. Maybe Hal would spurn my efforts, make me feel a fool.

I clicked on a reading light, blinking the room into focus. "Hal," I called.

I walked into the bedroom. "Hal."

The bed was unmade but empty.

I tapped on the bathroom door, then opened it. Empty.

I felt my stomach knot. Walked shakily to the closet.

Hal's clothes were gone.

I sank to the floor.

So much for trying. So much for talking.

I closed my eyes, pretending Hal was beside me. Pretending I could feel him there, smell his skin, hear his voice. Pretending those things meant being close to him.

Maybe Hal was just more honest than I was.

Exciting
MYSTERIES
With A Legal Twist
by
Lia Matera